Jessie is Her Name

Jessie is Her Name

✦

A Virginia Family's Oral History 1912-1949

A Novel

Don L. Brown

iUniverse, Inc.
New York Lincoln Shanghai

Jessie is Her Name
A Virginia Family's Oral History1912-1949

iUniverse books may be ordered through booksellers or by contacting:

iUniverse
2021 Pine Lake Road, Suite 100
Lincoln, NE 68512
www.iuniverse.com
1-800-Authors (1-800-288-4677)

Certain characters in this work are historical figures, and certain events portrayed did take place. However, this is a work of fiction. All of the other characters, names, and events as well as all places, incidents, organizations, and dialogue in this novel are either the products of the author's imagination or are used fictitiously.

ISBN-13: 978-0-595-42391-0 (pbk)
ISBN-13: 978-0-595-86727-1 (ebk)
ISBN-10: 0-595-42391-4 (pbk)
ISBN-10: 0-595-86727-8 (ebk)

Printed in the United States of America

This book is dedicated this 14th of February 2006 (Valentine's Day) to the love of my life, Carolyn Lee Mitchell Brown, my wife. It was through her hard work that this manuscript was finalized and without her inspiration and support, this book would never have been completed.

JESSIE IS HER NAME

◆

A Family History

Prologue

An early childhood story told to me by my brother Jimmy colored my view as a child. One day I was telling him how that Ronnie Whitson had gotten a "real electric train" for Christmas and how I got an "old wooden, hand made train" from our father and that mine had to be pushed around the floor and that Ronnie's made smoke and whistled and everything.

Jimmy was six years older than I and had as little to do with me as he could, but he looked at me and at the train made out of love by my father and said' "You know what, I would have loved to have had that train you got from dad when I was your age."

And then he told me a story that would affect the way I would think about my life forever. Jimmy said that when he was four or five, he was awakened from his sleep by the muffled steps and whispered conversations of our father. It was the night before Christmas and Jimmy thought that dad had come to get him up to come downstairs because Santa Claus had come.

Instead, dad stood in the open doorway with a coal oil lamp in his hand and said, "Jimmy, put your shoes on, grab your teddy bear and get on down stairs, we're leaving." He said he rubbed his eyes, saw dad there with his coat on and wondered what could cause father to get him out of his handyman's half-bed next to the warm flue if it wasn't for Christmas. And why did he have his hat and coat on?

What Jimmy did not know was that it was December 24th, 1937 and although the Great Economic Depression had long passed most areas of our country, its' grip was still strong on the small towns and villages of the Shenandoah Valley where he and our family lived. Men were still out of work, factories were still closed, and women were still lining up each morning at the coat factories and textile mills for just a chance at some piecework. Anything to earn a little money, pay the rent, feed the kids, to survive.

Later, I would hear from my mother how my father had suffered during this time. How he had worked three jobs at once in order to hold his family together. How with bloody, blistered hands he had come home at night to work in his garden so that he and his wife and his five sons could eat. So that our family would not have to "break up house-keeping."

As my father stood there in that half-light, Jimmy would say he knew nothing of this, he only knew he was being fetched out of his warm bed onto the cold bare floors of our drafty, uninsulated rent house, and he was afraid.

Socks on, shoes on, he grabbed for Theodore, his bear, and down the stairs he went. Standing at the bottom of the stairs, he could see our mother, coal oil lamp in hand, trying to illuminate the bottom of the stairs. Jimmy said she turned, and that silver streak in her matted brown hair pointed down towards her tired and scared face. My mother reached her hand out to Jimmy and before he could ask what was happening, mother said, "Now you be quiet child, everything will be all right." It was then that Jimmy said that he could see the pile of furniture on the front porch, our chairs, our sofa, boxes with dishes and clothes tied together in bundles.

Jimmy told his story and I could feel a tightness in my throat and a sense of embarrassment for what I had said about dad's hand-made Christmas gift. I had somehow missed those kinds of times that Jimmy was now describing and although I didn't know it at the time, I was being introduced into how past generations of our family had lived; about this midnight moving of one's belongings so that my father could be saved the indignity of having to hand haul all this stuff in the light of day.

So Jimmy said, there they were, all of his brothers, all older than him, with chairs on their backs, the round oak dinner table being carried in two pieces; the base by my oldest brother Charley, and the heavier base by the next oldest, Billy.

As Jimmy finished his story, he just soft tapped me on my head and as he made his way out the door, he turned and said, "Donnie, you don't know how good you have had it. I've had to move at least five times in my life and you haven't had to move once. You better thank your lucky stars for what you do have, and if I was you, I wouldn't mention anything about that train set that Ronnie got."

I have never forgotten that story that my now dead brother told me those many years ago. The 1940's would prove to be no picnic for the Brown family either but I would experience in those first ten years of my life all of those events that would define who I was, what I thought, and how I viewed my life.

The effects of poverty upon a young person cannot be quantified. In some, it causes such deep scarring that a person so affected can become mean and bitter and question why such a fate has befallen them. In others, it is just simply viewed as what life has handed you and you work to make the most of it. I think I fell somewhere in between. I was always acutely aware that I was born into poverty but because of the effect that certain people had on my life, the more cynical and angry response never really developed in me and my life has been so much better because of those people. Those people who have painted upon my canvas of life, this is their story.

1

"The summer of 1949"

The year, 1949, was the best year of my life. Oh, 1947 and 1948 had been pretty good too, but 1949 is that year that incorporated so many of my memories of my "growing up" years. And the best part of 1949 was June, July and August. Those months and what happened in those months continue to color and illuminate my life. Even today.

We were living at 231 North Lewis Street in one of Mr. Fallon's rent houses and I thought that old house was the center of the universe. All my brothers were home then, my father's health was good, and he was the quiet master of his house, his garden, and his brood. Momma was able to stay at home and not work out of the house. Grandma would come into town and stay with us during the winter and cook and tell stories. Yep, it was a great time. Christmases seemed better and life seemed better. We had won the war, we had not yet started talking about nuclear destruction and in that small time space, my life seemed better than it ever had been.

June was the Kiwanis Little League Baseball, chasing crawdads in the creeks of Gypsy Hill Park, building huts in the woods across from our house and having my brothers introduce me to a passion that I was to enjoy all my life. Western Movies.

July was July 4th and it's celebration with the parades, the band concerts, fireworks, picnics and family reunions. My first train ride to

Washington D.C. would happen that July and my very first major league baseball game.

August would be the time each year that I would go out to stay with my grandmother in the country at her little place by the creek. It was during that time I would learn to really love this old lady with her wisdom and her passion and her secrets.

Staunton, Virginia in 1949 was a small city of some twenty thousand people going through its post-war revival. New stores were opening, old warehouses were being targeted for replacement and talk was going on about having to replace some of the older city public schools. Brick sidewalks were being replaced with concrete ones and larger electric lines were being put up. It was a town alive with promise. It had been called the "Queen City of the South" and because of it's seven hills, the "Athens of the South." Clearly marked off between the wealthy, middle and lower classes, there was no problem of personal identification. You pretty much knew where you stood in Staunton and I don't remember any discussions in our house of upward mobility or being put down by some kind of "glass ceiling" above which we could not rise.

An example of what you could do with your life if you worked hard lived in our house in my father. All you had to do in 1949 was to walk down town with him and you could see how loved and respected he was in this place. Whether it was Sunday and you were in the First Baptist Church, or down at his work place, the Augusta Furniture Store, or at the firehouse where he was an air-raid warden during the war, or at Hagwood's Drugstore, anywhere you went you could see it in the way that people responded to him. He had, through the way he had lived his life, become an example of one who had climbed out of a lower economic caste and had provided for himself and his family in an honorable way.

That June started off hot and it stayed hot throughout the summer. That meant screens on the windows and screens on the doors and a constant checking to see if the spring on those doors were pulling the doors closed. There were repeated lectures about slamming the screened doors because you know "That causes the door to bounce back and let all kinds of bugs in." If I heard that banging of the screen door, followed by the lecture once, I heard it a hundred times as six boys and their friends went in and out of that old rent-house that summer.

Friends were a major part of that summer of discovery for me as Jake Armstead, Boyd Sinclair, Kirk Brannon, Gary Cosby, George Johnson and sometimes Ronnie Whitson made up a group of kids known simply as the "Lewis Street Gang." There were no formal rules to being in the gang except one. Do not tell your parents what we are doing, will be doing, are planning on doing, or wish we could do.

The gang's hideout was a fairly mobile home that we called "the hut". It was at various times composed of an old iron bed frame, some sticks of wood that we "acquired" from the back of the Coiner Parts Automobile Parts warehouse and cardboard of various widths and sizes. This "really good hut" was usually covered with either an old tarp we had "found" over at Central Tire Company on Central Avenue, or various pieces of linoleum that were carried four blocks from the trash dump behind where my father worked at the furniture store on Augusta Street. Where we got the old rug that remained for at least four years as the hut floor, I don't recall.

So in June, four or five little kids aged twelve, for Jake, to eight, for me, could be seen setting out for the woods every morning with building materials, a borrowed hammer and some nails, a can of potted meat, a few crackers and a bottle of Nehi pop or a thermos of water.

At certain times that hut was supreme allied headquarters for the Virginia infantry volunteers, Fort Lewis on the Brazos with a full compliment of horse soldiers with their stick horses, Space Station One—Buster Crabbe in charge. What wonderful days!! With awesome enthusiasm we depicted whatever adventure we had seen the Saturday before at the Strand or Visulite theaters. We were cavalry officers with whittled stick swords. We were Indians attacking a stagecoach that looked suspiciously like Ronnie Whitson's Radio Flyer wagon with a cardboard box on it. With homemade bows and arrows, we peppered that coach until no one could have survived.

Sometimes, as children are wont to do at that time and this, we would push the fantasy envelope. So many times, for us, that meant the use of fire in one way or another.

So, Flexible Flyer wagons were set ablaze and quickly put out with the only water we had to drink. Eyelashes were singed as we found out that powder removed from shotgun shells should not be thrown into a campfire regardless of how many times we saw Sunset Carson do it on the silver screen.

The leader of this highly dangerous gang of desperados was one Jake Armstead. His mom and dad ran the restaurant/bar over on Central Avenue. They lived upstairs. All of his brothers and sisters were much older so Jackie, the youngest, pretty much got away with murder. Mr. and Mrs. Armstead always seemed so involved in their place of business that was opened six days a week, nine to eleven, that they didn't really seem to take much interest in Jake. This resulted in Jake growing up pretty much on his own, and the head of our gang. His greatest two leadership skills focused around him being older and bigger than the rest of us and that because he could go into the restaurant any time he wanted, he had a pretty open-ended opportunity to provide the gang with an on going supply of potato chips, raw hotdogs, bread and eventually our first bottle of ice cold Pabst Blue Ribbon Beer.

He also had the first bicycle. A beautiful red one, horn in the middle section, separate lights, front and back, shiny fenders, a to-die-for bicycle. He smoked the first cigarette and told the first dirty joke. I didn't understand it, but I laughed anyway,

Because his brothers had been in the service, they knew how to cuss real good. Through Jake we all learned during that summer how to cuss real good too. He was a big, fat kid that always reminded me of that Hollywood kid actor of the '30s, you know, the one that got in some kind of trouble.

Day would begin for myself and the rest of the Lewis Street Gang when Jake arrived at my house and the rest of the guys, seeing Jake's bike, would all come a running. It was that way for almost four years, particularly for summers from 1947 through 1950 when it would all end.

But of all these years, 1949 was the best. June was always baseball, and I don't know how we did it, but all of us guys on Lewis Street played ball for some part of every day in that open lot next to our house on 231 North Lewis. The "field", as we called it, was just an open lot maybe sixty yards wide, bordering on Lewis Street and sixty yards deep backing up to the bus terminal lot and the Central Tire Company lot. In this space for four summers we played ball—baseball, football, stickball, ringball—whatever kind of ball we could come up with.

Well, one day, having acquired a brand new Titalist golf ball, we were able to prove that with one well-placed hit off of our 100% ash Adirondack baseball bat, that a golf ball could easily travel 180, maybe 190 feet and lodge in a second story fan blade on the top of the poultry processing building, clean across Central Avenue. Over the top of six Greyhound busses, over my Dad's garden, and way past my Mom's full clothes line!!

That day also proved that if five boys stay hidden all day in a bed frame hut covered with grass and leaves, that the police don't really come even though any abrupt approach of a policeman for years afterward would conjure up a sense of dread and the prospect of a long prison sentence.

The formal baseball training we would receive came through the auspices of the Staunton Kiwanis Club Little League Baseball Program. Every spring, boys from all over Staunton, West Augusta, Gospel Hill, Sears Hill, and downtown came together for the ultimate rite of spring—baseball.

The two city fields sat between the hills and creeks of Gypsy Hill Park and this green space created a romp space for everyone who entered in. If it was not playing in the creeks, it was swinging on the city park swings, or looking at the ducks and the swans at the duck pond. Huge goldfish and carp kept the pond's duck population in check and many a day we would spend watching a big old fish trail a young mother duck and her brood until the fish would break the surface of the pond and with a huge gulp, have a little duck sandwich and return to the bottom of the pond as we would stand there and marvel.

Ballgames began at 9:00 a.m. but the real games began at about 6:00 a.m. when Boyd Sinclair, Kirk Brannon, Bucket Richardson and Billy Snider would show up at my house ready to "get to the park".

On old bicycles, often riding double, with ball gloves hanging off the handlebars, we would make our way to the park to get ready for our game. With black-taped baseballs and wood-screwed old bats, we would play amongst ourselves for hours hitting and running and diving on the sand infield making catches that Bobby Brown of the Yankees would be proud of.

By the time the "official game" would begin, we would be so dirty and sweaty that the coach would sometimes ask: "What in the world have you boys been doing?" We would wear the same Kiwanis Little League shirt every day and by the end of the season, the combination of day-long play and hot water washes had the shirts looking pretty bad. Right off the bat, I recognized that there was a great difference between the kids that I played with and the sons of the "elite" of Staunton who delivered their children to the games in cars and sat in suits on the hill to watch the games. These children had cleats while we had ripped-up dirty tennis sneakers with taped up toes. They had new gloves with the smell of Neat's Foot Oil bought from Nick's, The Sportsman Sports Store, while we played with old three-fingered gloves with redone leather laces and tape on the palm to hold the padding in.

Everyone played for the chance of winning the league championship or being named an "All-Star". These two designations resulted in the greatest gift any young kid could get, particularly a poor kid like me; the reward of being taken on a Quick-Livick bus trip to Washington, D.C. to see a Washington Senators professional major league baseball game at Griffith Stadium!!

The year 1949 was the year that I would be named to the All-Star Team and for two weeks before we were to go, the other guys in the Lewis Street gang acted real strange. Instead of coming over to my house to congratulate me, in the morning they would meet at George Johnson's house at the edge of our woods and decide, sometimes before I got there, what we were going to do on that particular day. I noticed right off that after I made the All-Star team that the rest of the guys were a whole lot less interested in playing ball and that I seemed to be the only fellow who continued to wear my Kiwanis Little League shirt every day.

Oh, there was still a lot to do and soon I, too, forgot about ball as we discovered new things to do in this summer of discovery.

Some mornings we would all walk down Lewis Street and cross over Central Avenue at the firehouse and make our way to the alley behind the Spaulding Bakery building. Here, they made the most wonderful glazed donuts known to man. Years later, having tried Krispy Kreams, Holsoms, Merita, or Entemens donuts, there still is nothing like the smell that came out of that big fan that blew those fresh hot donut odors out into that alley as four little boys wished for a nickel so that they could go into the front of the bakery and there, on wax paper covered shelves, could purchase one of those huge, warm, succulent donuts.

We would sit there under the fan and smell those smells until we almost couldn't stand it anymore. It was always Jake who had the nickel and having all of us believe he didn't have a nickel that particular day, would suddenly jump up and run down the street to the corner of the Spaulding building and enter in. We would all run after him and, getting to the corner, would peer in, as Mrs. Jacobs would lift up the wax paper to let Jake make his choice. Now, with donut in hand, Jake would lead the gang back to our woods where, after a long, long time, he would take out his Boy Scout four blade knife and begin to cut this beautiful, warm, sugar glazed confection into four or five parts, depending on how many guys we had that particular day. Jake's piece was always larger but somehow that seemed right and after having us all swear undying love for him, he passed out the pieces of the donut.

Dinners at Maxims, The Four Seasons, and The Greenbrier would all be a part of our lives but nothing and I mean nothing, ever tasted so good and so wonderful as those warm five-cent donuts in that card-board hut in those Lewis Street woods in the summer of 1949.

About 5:20 every afternoon my dad could be seen walking up Lewis Street from his job at the Augusta Furniture Store carrying his lunch box. He laid carpet and made Venetian blinds, he put up linoleum walls in bathrooms and did special carpet projects for Churches and theaters. He was well respected, as I said, and I really loved seeing him come home in the afternoon because it meant I would have a little bit of his time. He would always come home, wash up and before supper, he would go out behind our house and work in his garden. It was during this time, this quiet time that I would talk to him, listen to him and just watch him. None of my brothers and none of my friends had the kind of relationship with their dad that I had with mine and my life has been so blessed because of it.

My father always worked very hard and my mother made sure that everyone knew what a good man her Luther was. But without the stories, without the accolades, he was special and you didn't have to be around him long to know it.

His sense of fairness, his ability to read people, his uncommon sense of problem solving; all were qualities that I admired in him in 1949 and would admire in him until his death in 1968.

He was 51 years old in 1949, but he seemed older and wiser. So, after he washed up, I would always try to be on the back steps of the house as he made his way to the garden.

"How are you doing, young man?" he would say as he ran his hand across my head and made for his special place of peace, his garden.

I learned real early that my father didn't like "mouthy people" and so I would quietly follow him down the backyard path to where he was going to work. There I would turn an old apple crate over and watch as this man, this graceful old man would hoe, and pick, and weed, and water his special quarter-acre lot.

I wouldn't know for years that the produce out of this garden; the beans, the tomatoes, the potatoes, and the corn had in some years meant the difference in being fed and going hungry. Of all the things he loved to do, and the things that gave him the most pride, working with his hands in that garden was his favorite. It kept us fed and as he would say "Keeps the wolf from our door."

I didn't know that until later, all I knew was that when my dad was working in his garden on a summer day, he was the happiest that I would ever see him.

There would be little interludes there during those afternoons when he would stop, and taking his red bandana out of his pocket, would walk back to where I was sitting at the end of the row where he was working. "Boy, run up and get me a dipper of water off the porch please," he would say. Even though there was a water standpipe at the end of his garden, he always seemed to like to see me run up to the house and get him a dipper of water out of the bucket on the porch.

Returning with the water, dad would ask me what I had done that day as he drank the water. I always gave him the sanitized version of what I had done because I had found out very early that he really didn't want to know "all I had done" with the day.

He would say something like "That's good son", and then oftentimes he would launch off into a story about his youth that always seemed to begin with "When I was a young boy like you—." They were great stories that have been told hundreds of times since to my children, to baseball teams and even during management training courses that I was to teach later in my life.

There were stories of growing up poor in Staunton at the turn of the 20th century, stories of Ku Klux Klan hangings and World War I soldiers marching on Washington. There were depression era stories and the running of electric lines in Staunton, of old tin fliver cars and having, as a boy, seen Buffalo Bill Cody ride around a sawdust ring at the Staunton Fairgrounds.

These stories seemed so special as told by this wonderful man who seemed to have so much to say but for the most part of his life would remain a very quiet, private person. Years later, when I would tell my brothers stories my dad had told me, they were amazed, as they had never heard them nor did they know that man who used to sit on that apple crate in that garden and tell me stories of his youth.

So, between the baseball, the jaunts to the park, the adventures of the Lewis Street Gang, and afternoons with my dad, the summer of '49 went past rapidly. August would come quickly that year and the time for my yearly visit to another of those special people of 1949, my grandmother, Althea Rowhema Rohr Campbell, would come.

My grandmother lived out in the country in a little valley area between Craigsville and Goshen, Virginia in a small three-room house with porches all around near a small creek. She would live out her life having never traveled more that 100 miles from her home.

I went there, I thought, because that's what you did. You went to visit your grandmother every summer. There was great shock for me in later years when I found out that none of my older brothers had gone to visit her and that none of the Lewis Street Gang knew much about their grandmothers either. When I heard in my later years that no one had the adventures I had experienced with my grandmother I felt very sorry for those people who had never had the wonderful times I had in those years 1946 through 1949.

My grandmother was a thin, country, woman who smoked a corn cob pipe, baked the best homemade bread in the world, had the most wonderful humor, could tell the greatest stories, and kept a family secret that would last almost 88 years.

My grandmother was my mother's mother and she had later married a fellow named Frank Campbell and thus my mother's maiden name was Jessie Mae Rohr while my grandmother's name was Campbell. Since it was 1949 and I didn't know anybody who was divorced or remarried, this name business always seemed strange to me.

It was then that on one evening, as grandma and I sat on the back porch looking out on the little creek that bordered her place that I decided to ask her once and for all about this "name business." She was packing her pipe with her "Prince Albert out of the can" tobacco when I asked her and she seemed to take an awful long time to answer me. Sitting herself down in her old hand-made rocking chair with the splat back and the curved arms, she finally responded. "Your mother's father and my first husband were named James Rohr, Donald", she said. "I married early, had Jessie early and then he left me. That is about all there is to it. Then I married Frank and we have been married ever since."

That would be the end of that story until 1993 when the real story of my mother's birth and her early adoption would be fully explained. But on that night in the summer of 1949, with my grandma and me on that back porch, there would be "bigger fish to fry." I had to learn about my uncle Ed, grandma's brother and how he once sold a one-eyed horse to a "city slicker" from Harrisonburg one day at the Farmer's Market in Staunton. I wanted to hear how my grandmother had been born with what the old folks called "A veil in front of her face" and as such, could "divine the signs", "make prophecy", and be known in later years as the "witch woman of the Estaline Valley."

As she launched into those stories, I would lean back against that old clapboard house and imagine a time when railroads were being built, "electric was coming to the country", and when wildcats and bears roamed and raided smoke houses.

She was seamless in her story telling. From the descriptions of the people, many of them long dead, to the actions that colored and illuminated my imagination.

It was also then that I learned something else about this gentle, kind, funny old woman. I learned that she had been the top speller in her class when she was in the 6th grade and as a product of a classic Latin education, she could purse out any word and spell it beautifully. Not only could she tell you the derivation of the word but also what it meant. Years later, when I would come home to Staunton to visit my mother and father while I was in graduate school, I would bring along a really bright student from school and after introducing them to my elderly grandmother, I would ask them to ask her to spell a word. They would haltingly give her a single-syllable word, not wishing to embarrass her. She would smile, pull one of her ever-present handkerchiefs out from her dress sleeve and proceed to sound out the word, spell it, and then tell the unsuspecting scholar the derivation of the word. A harder word would follow and another and before the visit was completed, she would quote him poetry, define the ideas of Hobbes and Locke, the writings of Charles Dickens, The Immortal Bede, and a whole slew of long-forgotten Greeks and Romans.

I could listen to her forever because she was truly a savant. She had been reading for so long when I met her that she had a first-hand knowledge of all the classic literature. She knew poetry and the thing that I would always remember, she would tell the stories of Romulus and Remus, of Robin Hood and the golden cities of Cibola with such passion and clarity. She had read the books, but more than that, she had ingested them so that in a throw-back to a time when reading was that one great escape, she traveled in those texts back in time and to places and cultures thousands of miles away from that back porch of hers next to the creek.

Being the youngest child of the six Brown boys, she always treated me differently. My brothers would never be encouraged to get an education like she would encourage me. They would never know her secret world of allusion, history, philosophy and art like I would and they would be the sorrier for it.

Walking with her over to Kinzer's store to get a piece of "store candy", my grandmother would open up her sows' ears purse and, while paying for my treat, would ask if any books had been dropped off by the train that day. That's how she got her education and would continue to grow and learn all through her life—off the train.

She had learned, as a young girl, that William & Mary College, a wonderful college in Williamsburg, Virginia, had a book lending program for rural people where-by you could simply put a request in the mail sack at Kinser's Store and when the train picked up the mail sack as it roared by, that book request would be filled if possible and the chosen book dropped off on a 14 day loan when the train dropped off the mail sack on it's return trip.

For all those years, as a young girl, a young woman, and now as a blessed grandmother, she had read and filled her life with the wonderful stories she would tell that small grandson who would fall asleep listening to her on that summer back yard porch.

Waking up to the smell of fresh baked bread, the sound of chickens in the yard and the bellowing of Sarah, the milk cow, served as such a juxtaposition to my life in one of John Fallon's rent houses on Lewis Street in Staunton that I found myself trying to savor every moment, to catch every new thing that happened. From chasing crawdads in the spring house to playing cowboys on the hill behind grandma's house, to feeding the two hogs, to picking apples for the apple butter—these summers served to show me that there were other things to do, other places to see, and in these summer days with grandmother, I was given an insatiable thirst for life that has lasted all my days. Without those days and this wonderful woman painting on my early canvas of life, I know my life would have been quite different.

2

"How much coal do we have?"

On a cold, wet, windy day in November 1935, a man made his way down Central Avenue in Staunton, Virginia towards Beverley Street. It was the worst of times as the economic collapse in America had resulted in more than just the closing of plants, the loss of jobs, and the breaking up of families. It had caused people to lose that most essential of human qualities, the ability to hope.

As this man walked on, clutching at his worn old brown coat, one could see the tatters on his pants cuffs, the patches on his sleeves and yet, in those beautiful clear eyes one could also see a sense of dignity and of purpose.

He rounded the corner of Central and Beverley Streets at the town clock building and made his way east on Beverley past shops now closed. Looking back over his shoulder up Beverley, he crossed the street to the two bronze doors of the Valley National Bank. The man put out his hand and attempted to pull the door open but it would not budge. He looked up at the town clock face and seeing it was 10:00, he wondered why the bank was not open.

The wind now blew up the street even harder as the first snow began to fall. The man turned again to the bank entrance and this time he could see the white paper flapping on the door. He pressed the paper flat against the door and tried in vain to read what was written there. This worn down little man with the fifth grade education standing in the cold before these huge bank doors seemed for one blinding moment as a metaphor for all that was happening at the time. No jobs, no money, the cold of winter, small children huddling in cold houses and apartments, homes being broken up to save the children, men and women working two and three jobs just to survive, little social welfare, little hope.

The snow now was blowing hard against the bare hand that struggled against the locked bank door. The man turned and saw another figure walking across the street from the bank. He turned and made his way toward the other person who was dressed warmly in his high collared, long black wool coat. "Mr. Lang, Mr. Lang", the poor man cried out. The businessman looked up from under the brim of his hat and seeing the man said, "Luther, what can I do for you?" "Mr. Lang," the poor man said, "could you please come across the street and tell me what that piece of paper says that's on the door of the Valley Bank?"

Mr. Lang recognized the man as a person who had purchased a ring at his jewelry store and someone he knew to be a good person, a hard worker, and by the looks of him, a man who was suffering with the times.

"Sure Luther, lets go see what it says," and with that the two men walked back across the wet, snowy street to the bank.

The jeweler pressed the white notice against the door and read the words: ANNOUNCEMENT—This bank is hereby declared to be temporarily insolvent. Signed Hershel Harris, State Treasurer.

The words tumbled from Mr. Lang's mouth and struck the shivering poor man as if he had been shot with a gun at close range. "What does that mean Mr. Lang?" the man asked. "It means that there is no money in this bank anymore, Luther." "No sir, it can't mean that, sir!" And with that, he pulled out an old black bank pass book and holding it up in front of the jeweler, he said, "I have been putting money in this bank since I was fourteen years old. I have $3,023.25 in that bank! It cannot be closed. I have done nothing wrong. I have been a good person. I have worked all my life for that money so that my children will not have to live hand-to-mouth as I have, so that we can have a roof over our heads and so that my children can have a home that is really theirs!"

Spontaneous tears were now rolling down the face of this desperate man who looked older than his thirty-seven years. With a look of total despair he held the passbook up to the businessman and said, "See, it's in here, it has to be in here!" "I'm sorry Luther" is all Mr. Lang could say. Putting his hand on his shoulder and avoiding the poor man's face, he quickly moved across the street, opened the door to his jewelry store and went inside.

Later, Mr. Lang would tell others that Luther must have stood there facing the locked bank doors for another twenty minutes as people walked by, cars passed and the wind, rain and snow continued to beat down upon him. Finally the man placed the black bankbook back inside his pocket and turned from the bank and started up Beverley Street toward home.

As he trudged along he thought about what the idea of a home had always meant to him. In his youth, Luther Brown's home had always been in one rent house after another. It had usually been down some hollow or on the wrong side of the railroad tracks. He had worked since he was nine at one make-do job or another. From sleeping three across in a bed, to rags or hand-me-down clothes, he had steadily marched onward until at the age of twenty he had become a celluloid-collar wearing sales person for the Banner General Store.

Now as he walked along facing into the snow, Luther let his mind drift off to those earlier times. He could once again see himself as a young man, a store clerk in the old Banner General Store. There, with pleated pants and a store bought shirt, he had looked successful even if he had to return each evening to that dilapidated, four-room row house down at the bottom of Kalorama Street. There Luther was just one of the seven poor-white Irish Brown boys.

Much of his pay at that time had gone to his home, but early on Luther chose a bank account over booze and the Baptist church over carousing and his reward for that was often times being told that he was trying to live "above his raising."

It was during this time, the spring of 1922 that his life changed forever. As he would walk home from work he would stop at Bowman's store and buy an apple and then proceed to eat the apple before he got home.

One evening as he was walking down Kalorama Street, past the beautiful old homes, fantasizing about what it must be like to live in such a house, he spotted a young girl on the porch of the house at the corner of Kalorama and Coalter Streets. She was beautiful, totally above him, and stunning. Her long brown hair was twisted in a bun and she was wearing a blue crushed velvet dress with a choke collar. Later he would say she looked just like one of those Gibson Girls from the magazines. She was standing at the end of the porch and she saw this thin, handsome young man coming down the street and after having looked his way she turned her face away and seemed to concern herself with an unruly tassel on her dress. This could just have been a chance encounter and soon forgotten had it not been for the fact that Luther, now pretending to be looking straight ahead, walked right across Coalter Street into the path of an oncoming trolley! "Luther, look out for God's sake," the trolley man screamed in his harsh Irish brogue. Luther looked up, jumped back as the trolley careened on down Coalter street hill with his uncle Clarence, the motorman, ringing the bell and shaking his fist at his erstwhile nephew.

Luther stood there and even though no more than three people had seen the incident, he felt the redness in his face and jumpiness in his throat that always attended an embarrassing moment for him.

Across the street he went, eyes straight ahead, all the while feeling the gaze of that pretty young girl on the porch of that big house on the corner.

For the next several weeks Luther would look out for her as he went to work and as he returned. As time went on that summer and he didn't see her, he thought that perhaps she had been a guest maybe at the house or a visiting relative and that he would never see her again. However, one day, as he was getting down a bolt of printed cloth for a customer, he heard Mr. Davis, his boss, say, "Well good morning Mrs. Strickland and to you Miss Jessie." Luther turned and there in the doorway with the early morning sun behind them was Mrs. Emma Strickland, the lady that lived in that house on Kalorama Street where he had seen the beautiful girl and next to her, that girl herself.

Luther would later tell others that he had really fallen for that young woman and to prove it, he had at that moment, stepped off the ladder into mid-air and fallen five feet to the floor throwing the gingham material across the store coming to rest at the feet of Mr. Davis. The young girl put her hand to her face to suppress her laughter as Mr. Davis and Mrs. Strickland looked on disapprovingly. "Luther, what in the world were you thinking?" Mr. Davis said, as he apologized to the other customers standing at Luther's case.

As Luther got to his knees, then to his feet, he could see his image in the long mirror on the back of the store's front door. His celluloid collar had sprung loose off his neck and now was sitting straight up behind his head. He looked like an Indian. Again, the red face and that nervousness came to his throat that resulted in his "I'm sorry" sounding like a small boy's cry.

Two moments, two incidents, "What must she think of me?" he thought as he busied himself cleaning up the mess and then it was back to the stockroom to straighten himself up. "God, Luther," he thought, "why didn't you just go over and start gagging in front of her or just fall down and start acting like you were tetched or something?"

When he returned to the front of the store they were gone but Mr. Davis wasn't. "Luther, I've always liked you and your father and I've always thought that you had a pretty solid head on your shoulders, so what I'm going to tell you now is for your own good. Luther, everyone has to know their place in this society and you need to know that your mooning over Miss Jessie like that is not good."

Luther could feel his chest tighten as he sensed the words that he felt were sure to come next. "The Stricklands are a well-established family in this town. Mr. Strickland is one of the best architects and house builders in Staunton. Mrs. Emma comes from old Virginia money, probably four generations or more, and Miss Jessie is their only foster daughter. They can't have any of their own."

Luther knew Mr. Davis was doing this for his own good. He had heard it before. "Stay with your own, don't get above your station, and know your limits." Luther knew well enough that he came from Irish rent-house poor but what about his dreams, Luther thought as he caught one last glimpse of Miss Jessie through the store window.

"Luther, are you listening? Now this is for your own good. There's nothing to be gained from an infatuation with a girl like Miss Jessie, so take this advice I give you and find someone of your own station. It will be better for everyone."

"Yes sir" is all that Luther could say. He needed this job. He had no education. He came from a poor side of town, of poor parentage. This job, with its' pay and the clothes and the courtesies he was afforded by Mr. Davis were a far cry from working in the chemicals of the tannery or the noise and dangers of the lumber mill where he had worked before. After all, Mr. Davis had taken a chance on even hiring him after having seen him and his father working at the church.

He would put her out of his mind. Just do a real good job and maybe one day Mr. Davis would make him manager of the store. Then with a position and a future he could perhaps think such high thoughts again. When the time was right.

For the next two weeks Luther took the back way home. Down Beverley to Augusta, right on Augusta, down Johnson Street past the gas house on Lewis Creek and cross the footbridge to the bottom of Kalorama Street and home. Each evening he would finish his apple at the creek and take the core and throw it in the stream. Then, he would stand there for a few moments and watch the apple drift down the creek towards the railroad tracks.

Later in his life he would recall how he would sometimes watch that core and pretend it was a boat and that he was on it and it was taking him far away from Staunton and his family and that pretty girl on the hill that he could not get out of his mind.

But it would be fate, not dreaming that would give Luther his opportunity to meet this girl and it was a fate that no one could have predicted.

The summer of 1922 became the fall of that year and with the coming of the first frost came the realities of living in a cold-water row house heated by a single coal stove. After stuffing paper into the open spaces in the clapboarding on the house, Luther, his father and his brothers, but mostly Luther, would cut and stuff burlap sacks on all the window openings and then nail the windows closed to be opened again in the spring.

The coal for the stove was another matter, as the price was determined, not by the poor of Staunton, but the rich of Staunton up on Gospel Hill.

To help with the coal, Luther always found himself working two jobs from September to February. First, he would go to work for Mr. Davis at the Banner store and then after changing out of his store clothes, he would go down and work shoveling coal in the boilers at the gas plant where his father was a boiler man. For twenty-five cents a day and a tote bag of coal a day, Luther would work from seven to ten each night on the job that no one else in Staunton wanted, that of a coal scooper for the gas boilers. After three hours of this backbreaking work, Luther would take his twenty-five cents and his tote sack of coal home. Washing up in a cold water flat after being knee deep in a coal pit took another hour and finally he would climb into that old tick mattress bed beside his brothers and fall off to sleep. These quarters would become the dollars that would be deposited in the Valley National Bank and on particularly hard days, Luther would take the bankbook out of it's hiding place on a shelf behind the kitchen stove and look at the growing total and dream those dreams that would sustain him.

So, it came to pass that on a cold winter night in November, 1922 that the stars would align in such a fashion that Luther, this hard working

Irish dreamer, would be at the right place at the right time to change his destiny.

Carrying the hod bag of coal on his back after finishing his shift, Luther was making his way up Coalter Street rather than the normal long way around Lewis Creek and across the footbridge as usual. He had nearly fallen in the creek the night before and so it was up Coalter, turn at the corner of Coalter and Kalorama, across the street from the Strickland's house and down Kalorama to his house at the bottom of the hill.

It was dark and cold as Luther started up the hill and he could feel the wind grabbing at his pants and pulling at his cap. With his head down and his back arched to support the bag of coal, Luther could not see what was happening up the hill ahead of him. For at that moment a fully loaded truck was coming down the ice-slickened Coalter Street hill. The ice on the trolley tracks were to be avoided at all costs and as the driver of the truck pushed on the brakes, he knew immediately that he was on those icy rails. He pumped the brakes again to gain control of the sliding truck that was piled high with wood but to no avail. The truck seemed to be literally shooting out from under him. He could sense the truck turning towards the right and the tail end starting to skid around to the left. He could hear the wood falling off the truck and knew that the vehicle was turning sideways to the hill and heading straight at the stonewall in front of the house at number 9 Coalter Street.

Luther heard the screeching of the truck tires and looking up, was startled to see a truck turning side ways on the street and with tremendous speed, flip over throwing the wood down the street towards where he was standing. Sparks flew from the side of the truck as it careened down the hill and straight into the wall at number 9 Coalter Street.

Luther dropped the bag of coal and ran in the direction of the over-turned truck. Just steps away from the accident, Luther could see the flames coming out from under the truck and could hear the cries of the driver within. He climbed to the top of the truck and as he would relate to others years later, he somehow was able to get the passenger side door opened and reaching down into the darkness of the truck, felt the out stretched arm of the driver. Quickly, Luther was able to get his arm around the injured man and with the strength that he would always be known for, hoisted the driver out of the truck. Carrying the man on his shoulders like a bag of coal, Luther quickly made his way across Coalter away from the accident and there in the light coming out of the door to Bob Palmer's house, saw for the first time the face of the driver. Douglas Strickland, Staunton house builder, the foster father of the pretty girl at 303 Kalorama!

3

"Don't Get Above Your Raisings"

"Lute, Hey Lute" the man was calling as Luther approached the door to the Banner Store the morning after the truck wreck. "I heard you saved old man Strickland last night." "Well, I just happened to be there," Luther replied trying to get the key in the lock. "Well, I heard he would have died if you hadn't pulled him out," the man continued as others came across the street from the two hardware stores. The hands on his back, the words of the crowd, were all like a heavy weight on Luther's shoulders. He was always a quiet man and he could feel his cheeks redden and even though early morning snow was falling, he could feel heat rushing up under his celluloid collar and he pulled at it with his hand to somehow cool himself down.

"Now what's all this commotion?" Mr. Davis was heard to say as he approached this gathering of people at the front door of his business. "It's Luther, Mr. Davis," cried Shorty Minter, the thick-bodied Ast Hardware clerk from across the street. "He's a hero, he's done saved Mr. Strickland from burning up in a truck accident."

Mr. Davis looked straight at Luther and smiled and then said, "Well good work Luther, I'm proud of you!" After what seemed an eternity, the group finally broke up and Luther, relieved, opened the door and he and Mr. Davis went inside.

All morning long people came into the store to hear the story and to offer praise and through it all, Luther could sense that the events of the night before somehow would change his life forever. He would be right.

The two spring-loaded doorbells rang at exactly 12:30 as Luther was on the ladder winding the eight-day store clock. At first Luther thought it was the clock chiming the half hour but the voice of a customer would tell him otherwise. "Young man, are you Luther Brown?" a very serious voice called out. "Yes Mam," Luther said as he backed down the ladder from the ledge where the clock was mounted. "Well, I'm Mrs. Douglas Strickland and I've come to thank you for saving my husband's life last night." Luther's knees went weak, as it always seemed to when he was faced with a social encounter with a person of station. He turned and there before him was Mrs. Emma Strickland, long black dress, high white lace collar, black hat, hair high on her head. Her clear eyes and well formed face and nose gave full notice she was indeed a person of station, of wealth, and of breeding.

She extended her gloved hand to Luther and in his frustration he offered his own hand, which had the clock key in it. Surprised by the key in the handshake, Mrs. Emma pulled her hand back and the key fell to the floor between them. Luther felt at that moment that she was looking right through him. This klutz, this low-stationed store clerk seemed to always be doing the dumbest things at the wrong time. "Excuse me," he said as he quickly retrieved the clock key from the floor. "Been winding the clock," he said nervously. "Obviously," she said as she fanned her hands and arms to shake the snow off her dress. It was at that moment he saw the open door and there in the opening was the most beautiful sight he had ever seen. It was Jessie.

He had seen her many times since that first day when his uncle had yelled at him from the trolley, but never this close up, never like this.

Her beautiful hair, long brown and silky shown from under her wide-brimmed hat. A pearl hatpin pierced the crown of the hat as if spotlighting her face. Her face was aglow, eyes flashing, beautiful teeth, and high cheekbones. She really did look like a Gibson girl from the magazines. He had been right the first time he saw her.

"Young man, have you heard a word I've said?" The words came to Luther as if from some other world. "Mam?" he said, still looking straight ahead at the young girl, this young, beautiful Jessie. "What I said was," Mrs. Emma continued, "was that we owe you a deep debt of gratitude for what you did last night." "It was really nothing Mam, anybody would have done the same thing," he said.

"No, young man, you're wrong. What you did was outstanding and when my husband is up and around again, he will see that you are compensated." The next few words that were to tumble out of Luther's mouth would be Heaven sent and change his life forever.

"Mam, I really don't need to be paid for doing what was the right thing to do." Luther could feel young Jessie's eyes upon him and in her face he could see her look of admiration. In that one glance he would see the response that he would try to recreate over and over for the next forty-seven years.

"Mother, why don't we ask Mr. Brown to supper on Sunday so that he could see how well Dad is mending?" the young girl said. "Jessie, I'm sure Mr. Brown has other plans that need to be considered before just agreeing to sup with us."

"No Mam" Luther almost shouted.

"No, you can't come or no, you have no other plans young man?" Emma inquired.

"No Mam, I have no other plans and would love to see you again. I mean I would love to have supper with you on Sunday, if that would be all right," Luther stammered wondering if Mrs. Emma had caught his youthful transgression of social decorum.

"Very well then, Sunday it is. Five o'clock." With this, Mrs. Strickland turned and, catching the look on Jessie's face, said, "Come Jessie, we must be off to pick up your father's prescription at Hagwood's." The two women left the store, gingerly stepping across the snow-covered street and heading downtown towards Hagwood's Drug Store in the next block of Beverley Street.

"BONG!" The town clock struck one and awakened Luther from his trance. He had been standing in the same place in the store looking down the street since the two women had left. Twenty minutes that he would years later recall were as if time had stood still so that he could breathe in the smell of her, the look of her, the idea of her.

The euphoria of the moment followed Luther throughout the day. Things done automatically suddenly were interrupted by moments of personal escape. It was indeed a good thing that Mr. Davis had been on business in Harrisonburg this particular day or he would have wondered about his judgment in leaving Luther in charge of his store.

It was only on the way home after he had closed up the store that the reality of Luther's situation struck him. What was he thinking? He didn't know how to eat in a fine house. What would he wear? Other than his coal worker's clothes, all he had to wear were clothes that Jessie had already seen on him in the shop. More pressing was what his mother would say. She always had admonished his brothers about "growing where you're planted" and being sure about "not getting above your raisings."

The poor Irish girls that his brothers Roy and Clarence had brought home seemed to fit his mother's idea of what was acceptable but not a blueblood like one of the Strickland's.

In later years he would recall how long that walk home had been through the snow and how he hated putting on those dirty coal workers pants that night. He knew how important he was to his family and based on past experience, he knew in the future his labors would still be needed.

The dullness of his gray poverty wore heavily on him all that week as he wished for a better family and a more promising future.

Wednesday passed, as did Thursday, Friday and Saturday. He took out $4.00 from his bank account for a new shirt and collar and a bottle of lilac water when he went to the barbershop that Saturday evening.

All of his purchases were hidden and his excuses made. Come Sunday he would cast off his lot if for just a few minutes. He would climb the hill from the town side, cross the trolley tracks, and have supper with the Stricklands. For one moment, he would be living "above his raisings."

4

"What are you going to do with the little girl?"

Looking back at the year 1912, Douglas Strickland would say that it had been the year that God had given him his only child.

The Stricklands were unable to have children and over a succession of years had "taken in" various children to fill the void of a childless house.

So, on that April morning in 1912 as he and his wife, Emma, made their way out of Staunton, there was no forewarning that their life was to change so dramatically. As their car careened and sputtered west along the Buffalo Gap road and the Esteline Valley road beyond, these two old friends talked and pointed out things to each other along the way.

Mrs. Emma, or Dotty as he called her, was a remarkably beautiful woman. A fourth generation Strickland, she had married a Strickland. The marriage to Douglas had not been well received by her parents who thought Douglas to be below them in station and not suitable. Mrs. Emma was known throughout her life as "a force to be reckoned with" and as being as strong willed as she was beautiful.

Taught all of the proper etiquette of the day by her very serious and social conscious mother, she was used to servants, big houses, and social gatherings of like-positioned aristocrats. She was a product of Southern Gentility four generations deep.

Douglas on the other hand was from, as he would say, "the poor side of the Strickland clan." A son of a Presbyterian minister, he and his six brothers were all trades people.

Early training as an architect, compliments of a Presbyterian scholarship, had not changed Doug from the hands-on type of fellow he had always been. He just loved to build things from fences to silos to carriage houses and finally to the calling he would be remembered for, a custom-house builder in Staunton and Augusta County. His homes would always be seen as the very best carpentry of the day. Beautiful raised paneling, exquisite dental moldings and finish trims always done to his high standards.

So, as this loving couple, now barren for sixteen years, drove along, they had established an equilibrium of understanding as to who they were and their relationship to one another. They stopped for gas at Kinzer's Store and as Mr. Strickland kicked the tires on his wooden spoked touring car and busied himself with checking under the hood, Mrs. Emma went inside.

There among the circles of cheese on wooden platters, canned goods stacked high on shelves, brine crocks filled with pickles for two cents apiece, patterned pieces of cloth laid open for inspection, Mrs. Emma sought out a delicacy far below her station. For there in the corner as it always was, was Mr. Kinzer's home made wine section. This is what she had come for. There one could find home made muscadine, dandelion, elderberry and blackberry wines. Wines that were drinking wines to these hill folks but to such an upstanding Presbyterian woman like Mrs. Emma, to be used for "medicinal purposes", you understand.

After selecting several bottles along with a number of other purchases, Mrs. Emma directed Mr. Kinzer to place the items into one of her collecting baskets, as they were called, and had him carry the baskets to the car.

Kinzer gave a "spin start" to the car and with a wave of his hand sent the Stricklands on their way west from his store towards the Estaline Valley and Goshen Pass.

Ostensibly this monthly trip was being taken to purchase farm goods in season that Mrs. Emma would have cleaned, cooked and canned for her winter pantry. Her husband, however, knew it had a much greater purpose. For it had been on such a trip that she and Douglas had first met and though suppressed in her youth, she was still a hopeless Victorian romantic who loved the thrill of visiting places that transported her to an earlier time. To the days of her now-passed youth.

Although the conversation centered on those things being seen and the beauty of this mountain valley, what she really loved was this feeling of freedom away from home, social schedules and the sameness of life. Often times she would ask Douglas to slow down to see a horse running free across an open field or to stop so she could sample water coming out of an artesian well next to an old dead oak tree.

It was 1912 and the condition of the roads varied greatly as they motored along from macadam to gravel to dirt and back again. Just as they approached the hill leading to the old Lebanon Presbyterian Church, Douglas heard the sound that all early motorcar owners hated—BANG! The right back tire blew and Douglas slowly pulled the car to the side of the road. He left the motor running and went to check the damage. The tire had blown clean off the rim, he told Emma, and getting back into the driver's seat, he explained that the

Rohr's home-place was just up the road and that he was "gonna run it on the rim" up to their house and fix it there.

Douglas knew Mr. Rohr very well, having bought chickens and eggs and sausage from him at the Farmer's Market in Staunton. He and Mrs. Emma had visited the Rohr home once formally during a religious retreat at Goshen Pass. Mr. Rohr was the superintendent of the Sunday school at Lebanon Presbyterian Church and well known in the Strickland's church circle of friends. He was also a very serious Christian fellow, Emma remembered. So, as the three-tired car turned into the lane leading to the Rohr's, she carefully covered the one basket filled with the "medicinal wines" she had purchased at Kinzer's.

The lane leading to the Rohr's house was tree-lined and marked carefully by a well-groomed chestnut railed fence. The house set on the side of a hill facing south with the barns playing out behind it in a beautiful meadow. Emma thought it looked like a picture of an American homestead from an earlier time.

Mr. James Isaiah Harrison Hite Rohr was a tall, lean six-footer with broad shoulders, well-trimmed beard and the natural movements of a man well used to the world of hard work. His 125-acre farm was his father's gift to him for staying at home when his other three sons had left the farm seeking jobs in Lexington, Roanoke and beyond. James had improved the place each year and the condition of the house and the barns spoke volumes of the long days and hard work he had put into it. Along with his farm, he had a reputation of being a first class boot maker and people often times would stop to inquire about the possibility of James Rohr 'building' them a set of boots.

But beyond all these accomplishments, James Rohr was most proud of his church work. He was constantly doing something for the church and the church community. As an elder and a deacon, he took his religious duty seriously and openly spoke out against the "evils of liquor and wanton ways."

As Douglas helped his Dotty out of the car, he heard the beautiful singing voice of a woman coming from the side porch of the house. As they approached they could hear, "Look over Jordan and what can you see—coming for to carry me home? A band of angels coming after me, coming for to carry me home." It was beautiful and as the Stricklands stepped up on the porch, the source of the singing looked up from her churning stool. It was Mary Elizabeth Glover Rohr, James Rohr's wife.

"Well, hello there," she said in her beautiful open country kind of way. She immediately recognized the Stricklands and, cleaning her hands off on her gingham apron, she extended her hand in welcome.

This juxtaposition of wealthy, plantation born Dotty and the woman of the homestead, Elizabeth, could not have better tied together the two totally different cultures, but in their eyes, one could see the admiration of two persons equally envious yet proud of each other's station. In Dotty, Elizabeth could see the cultured breeding of a classically raised southern sophisticated woman with position and power and place. In Elizabeth, Dotty could see the presence of person emanating from a beautiful, plain, dignified country lady, capable of child bearing and child raising, a keeper of hearth and home. Completely living her life as she wanted to live it.

James Rohr could be seen coming across the meadow so Douglas turned from the porch and walked down the fence line toward him. Carrying a young calf on his back, James looked like the mountain of a man that he was, dwarfing the small calf across his shoulders.

"Hey James," Douglas cried out. Hearing the call, James' very serious face broke into a huge smile on seeing Doug, a man he greatly admired. These two very good men had often talked about their lives, work and particularly about their religion, so the handshakes offered at the meadow gate were warm and honest.

Douglas told James of his predicament and the two men busied themselves with fixing the punctured tire while the two women made casual conversation on the porch.

Suddenly, around the corner of the porch came a small tassel-haired young girl all in gingham with bows flying in her hair and running at a gallop. She startled the two women and proceeded to crash into Elizabeth's churn sending it spinning towards the porch's edge. Elizabeth jumped up from her porch rocker just managing to catch the churn before it fell. Wide-eyed, this little dervish continued past the churn, bouncing off the house wall and around the corner of the house and out into the yard.

"Jessie, you come back here this minute!" came a call from around the porch as a young woman came into view in hot pursuit of the small girl. The young woman, probably about eighteen or nineteen years old, stopped cold in her tracks when she saw Mrs. Emma. "Oh, excuse me. I'm sorry," she stammered and as quickly as she had arrived, she withdrew around the house in the direction where the little girl had gone.

"Sorry, Mrs. Emma. Did any of the milk splash on you?" Elizabeth asked, looking equal parts annoyed and angry at what had transpired.

"No, not hurt a bit but who was that little girl? I've not seen her before on your visits to Staunton?" Dotty inquired.

"Well, you know you try to raise your children up right with the right kind of values, but sometimes the devil has a way of messin up your plans," Elizabeth said as she straightened her dress and apron and went over to sit down next to Dotty. "It's no secret here in the Esteline Valley that my daughter, Allie, got involved with a railroad tie cutter a few years ago and was "with child" with him. The man asked for Allie's hand but James would have nothing of it and sent the man packing. They say he left to go back over the Blue Ridge to his home in Ivy. It has not been easy on James, him being a deacon and a superintendent and all. It's the first trouble of this kind we've ever had in our family on either side. I can see James is really sufferin over it. He doesn't touch the little one and his attitude towards Allie has changed totally since it happened. I believe James would like the whole mess to just go away. It is really just eatin him up."

The words just flowed from Elizabeth's mouth and the candor and openness caught Dotty unaware as such conversations were seldom heard in her circle of friends and particularly not amongst social acquaintances such as she viewed her relationship to the Rohr's.

"What are you going to do with the little girl?" asked Dotty.

"Well, we'll probably send her up to the children's home in Covington come fall. Something's got to be done. She's got such spirit and she's constantly into stuff, as you have just seen. She's constantly running here and climbing there. She left the pen gate open last week and all the pigs got out and ran up into the woods. Took James half a day to get them all back."

With the tire fixed and the sun quickly starting to set, Douglas and James made their way up towards the porch where the two women had been sitting.

"You all will stay for supper, won't you?" James asked as they stepped up on the porch.

"Well, we better be getting back to Staunton," Douglas replied. "I've got a large order of wood that I have to pick up at Holsinger's Lumber Yard tomorrow and I really need to be there to start that house up on Sear's Hill next week."

A question asked and a question answered, the two women responded by standing and again extending her hand, Dotty said, "You two will have to let us know when you will be at Market again and James, I would appreciate it if you would save Mr. Strickland and I some of that wonderful tenderloin when you butcher again this fall."

"Will do, Mrs. Emma and I will bring you some cracklins and souse too."

As Dotty and Douglas made their way down the steps, she quietly whispered to her husband, "Douglas, there is the most beautiful little girl living here and they are going to take her to that dreadful place in Covington if we don't do something about it."

"What?" Douglas stammered. "What girl? I haven't seen any girl."

"Shush! Don't say anything. Let's get to the car first." Dotty whispered.

The couple hurried down the path to the car and turning and waving to the Rohrs, Douglas's eye wandered up and toward a second story window. There he saw a little face pressed against the windowpane. All curls, a poignant half-smile on her face, and a little hand slowly waving down at him.

Douglas would tell friends later on that at that moment he found the only daughter he would ever have. For there in the window was the tiny Jessie. He would say that it felt like he had been shot through the heart. Oh, he and Emma had had foster children before but never had he felt the feeling that he had that day as his eyes met that little face. Until he died in 1951, he would tell friends and strangers alike of this gift of God that came his way that day.

"Dotty, please sit in the car a minute, would you?" "Why, what are you going to do?" Emma said as she grabbed for Douglas's arm.

"Well, we don't have anybody but Gertrude back at the house in Verona. I'm going to see James about what he's going to do with that little girl."

As Dotty set there in the car with the sun setting over the mountain, she watched as Douglas and James walked down from the porch and, in deep conversation, started moving to the side of the house. They would stop every few feet, look at each other, and then continue until they were out of sight on the other side of the house.

After what seemed like an eternity, out of the front door came James, Elizabeth, and in Douglas's arms, the little girl. Two small tote sacks hung from her husband's arms. All the earthly possessions of that tiny six year old were now being brought towards Emma.

Suddenly Douglas stopped, and with the child in his arms, he returned to the porch steps and there he asked, "What's this little girl's name?" Elizabeth answered for them both by saying, "It's Jessie, Jessie is her name." Douglas looked down into that beautiful face and said, "Then Jessie it will be."

When he reached the car, Douglas said, "Jessie, this is Emma. Emma, This is Jessie," and gently he handed the child to his wife. Emma brushed the girl's curls away from her face and saw the tracks of her tears and felt the wetness on the little girl's collar. "It will be all right."

she said as she cradled her to her shoulder. Jessie's face, Emma would recollect later to friends, looked like the eyes of a deer caught in a fence; fearful, surprised, hurt and afraid.

As the car turned and started down the lane, Jessie turned in Emma's grasp and in the sunset light, she could see a figure running down the lane after the car. When the figure got to the little bridge, it stopped and Jessie could see the young woman in the road waving with one hand, her other hand across her mouth. Then, slowly, the figure was gone in the dusk. It would be another twenty-one years before little Jessie would see her real mother again.

5

"From ticken' mattress to a four poster bed"

To sleep on a tick mattress with cotton sheets and home made quilts one night and to awaken in an Antebellum southern mansion bedroom in a four poster testered bed, damask bed covers and more huge duck down pillows than you have ever seen is what little Jessie experienced after the Stricklands got her to their home in Verona, just east of Staunton.

She heard the house before she saw it. She was awakened at dawn by the sound of metal being drug up the back stairs and being placed down on the wide planked pine floor. The black house servant, Gertrude, opened her bedroom door and the first words Jessie heard were "Time to get up child!" She kept her head under the covers until Gertrude approached her bed and she could hear her say, "Well let's see what they done brought home now!" And with that, Gertie, as she was called, pulled the bed covering back away from Jessie's face to reveal, as Gertie would later tell others, "a mess of curls and eyes the size of buckeyes."

Gertie had seen lots of children come and go in the forty years she had served the Stricklands. Lost children, abandoned children, children from Strickland relatives, but never had she seen such a poor, scared, yet beautiful little wretch such as this.

She moved her long black, calloused hand toward the little girl and Jessie recoiled and pulled the covers back over her head. "Now come on child, ole Gertie's not gonna hurt you. I just want to see what Mr. Douglas and Mrs. Emma has brought me home this time."

Gertie's voice was soothing but straight to the point and when Jessie continued to hold the covers over her head, Gertie just gently grabbed the covers and with a quick pull, uncovered the little girl.

The early morning light was coming through the huge floor-to-ceiling east window with such brightness that Jessie covered her eyes and slowly, through her fingers, looked up at this huge black woman who was to become her great friend, teacher, confidant and in a real sense, in this very ordered household, her real day-to-day mother. Jessie would later in her life describe the Gertie she saw at this moment as this huge, black nanny with a bandana on her head, a great big white-toothed smile, huge hands on huge hips looking down on her as if she was a pork chop at the farmers market.

"Get yourself up outta there child. We got a mess of work to do to get you ready for Mrs. Emma. Come on now, we are burning daylight."

With those strong dark hands Jessie was lifted from the bed by the first black woman she had ever seen. Later, Jessie would relate to friends that she wanted to scream but was so afraid that the sound wouldn't come out of her mouth.

"Well just don't stand there Jeremy. Get that hot water in that tub like I told you," Gertie said, and for the first time, Jessie was aware that there was someone else in the room. There at the door stood a gangly, thin young colored boy with two buckets of steaming water that he had carried from the kitchen below Jessie's room.

"Yes mam. I'm doin it. I'm doin it," said the boy as he poured the water into the galvanized bathtub sitting at the end of the bed.

"Now get outta here child," Gertie said as she motioned the boy toward the door. With buckets in hand, the boy backed out of the room and pulled the door closed behind him.

"Now little ragamuffin, let's get you out of those things you got on and get you nice and pretty for Mrs. Emma."

Slowly, Gertie pulled the cotton shirt and drawers off the little girl as Jessie tried to cover herself as best she could. With a wave through the tub water, Gertie now picked Jessie up and ever so gently sat the child down in the nicest smelling water she had ever known.

"Magnolia, darlin," Gertie said as she saw the little girl react to the smell. "I made the soap myself off of blooms from that big ole magnolia out in the front yard yonder. My Mama taught me how when I was a young girl and she was taught by her momma, my grandmother, who was a house slave for Colonel Gardner before the war."

Gertie said all this while she moved the wash cloth over the child with one hand while lathering her up with the magnolia bath soap with the other.

"I've been with the Stricklands one way or another for almost forty years and my momma before me," she said as she continued to wash this newest addition to her home.

"Yessum, I could tell you some real tales about the people Mr. Douglas and Mrs. Emma have brought in here. They comes and they goes but old Gertie, she's still here."

How long the soap in her eyes had burned her, Jessie couldn't say but suddenly she started to cry. Gertie looked down at the crying child as if startled back to reality.

"Oh child, I'm sorry, ole Gertie is just a talking and washin you and done forgot where she was. Here child, let's get that soap outta your eyes."

"Gertie, what's wrong?" the question climbed the stairs. "Oh nothing, Mr. Douglas. Just some soap in her eyes, that's all." Gertie thought to herself that it was a good thing that it had been Mr. Douglas and not Mrs. Emma that had heard the cry, for she would have made Gertie explain herself for her actions.

Quickly now, Gertie swaddled the little girl in the two towels she had brought to the room. She carefully cleaned around the eyes of this new foundling and then it hit her, her eyes, they looked just like the eyes in that old locket that laid on Mr. Douglas' desk. Lord Almighty, she thought, a spitting image of that other little girl in the locket.

In later years, Gertie would tell friends she could feel the hair raise up on the back of her arm as she looked at that wet little baby and thought of what had happened to that other child, the one in the locket. Gertie said after the shock had passed, she held the child for at least fifteen minutes. Although she would watch after Miss Jessie for nine more years, she never felt closer to her than that morning with the sunlight walking across the floor of that old plantation house, the pile of home-spun clothes at her feet and that tiny baby girl in her arms.

6

"Living at the Mansion"

In 1940, my mother was taken to the Dixie Theater by my dad to see "Gone With the Wind" with Clark Gable. In later years my mother would say, "Who would have ever thought that I, as a young child, lived in such a house as Tara and had taffeta dresses like Scarlet O'Hara?" Then she would throw her head back, laugh and say, "Oh how the mighty have fallen!" But, back in 1912, walking down that circular staircase in her new dress with Gertie holding her one hand and with her other hand sliding down that beautiful, curving walnut handrail must have indeed felt like something out of the movies.

A six year old child, now smelling of magnolia, in a new dress, coming down the most wonderful staircase she would ever see—well, it must of seemed like a dream.

At the bottom of the stairs, Douglas Strickland was overcome. This wonderful, quiet, dignified southerner's eyes filled as Jessie came into view. What a good decision he and Emma had made, he thought. Taking a small child out of harms way, raising her in a Christian home, these were things that Douglas and Emma had done before. But little did he know that first morning that this curly-haired little waif would become the soul-child he had always hoped for.

Emma joined him at the base of the staircase and, though she saw the specialness of this child, she also saw her as a project. She was to be taught good manners, proper etiquette, needlepoint, the ways of run-

51

ning a household, and the treatment of servants. As she stood there looking up, Emma saw young Jessie as clay to be molded, a spirit to be directed. Little could Emma know where all of this insistence on decorum would lead.

"Well, here she is!" Gertie said as she attempted to let go of Jessie's hand. Feeling Gertie pull away from her startled Jessie and she looked furtively at the old black woman. "Here's your new folks, honey child," she said and turned to go back up the stairs. Jessie grabbed at Gertie's apron and a tiny "No" came out of her mouth. Perhaps that would be significant that the first word out of this headstrong young woman's mouth would be "No."

Douglas Strickland gently picked her up. "Gertie's got lots of things to do darling," he said to Jessie. "She will be right back down when she's done with her upstairs chores. Come on now, let me show you around your new house."

Douglas Strickland smelled good. That was the first thing my mother would remember about that first day at the Strickland mansion house. He smelled good.

Now firmly in his arms, she was given a tour of this beautiful early 19th century house. The shiny cherry floors, the chair rails, the raised paneled walls with their gold-rimmed oil paintings of Stricklands long passed.

The center hallway with its' huge marble tiles and gold chandelier. To the left was a dark paneled room with a high ceiling. Floor to ceiling windows were opened and the smell of gardenia and lilac filled the room. A huge roll-top desk and a painted world globe caught Jessie's attention. Instinctively she said, "What's that?" pointing at the globe. "That's a globe, honey," Douglas said, and with that he put Jessie down. Taking her hand, he walked her toward this painted round ball sitting in its' wooden nest. "Here we are honey," he said, pointing out the United States. Jessie put her little hand on the sphere, looked up at Douglas and said, "You're nice." Douglas Strickland, architect, builder, and self-made man, melted. Caught in that innocent gaze of that little curly-haired girl, he fell in love. It was to be a true love that would last for 38 years.

All that first day was spent in seeing things and touching things and smelling things. In later years, my mother would tell me of this first day at the mansion over and over again. With each telling you could sense her excitement, her sense of wonder.

Days at the plantation house would completely consume Jessie and she took to the life as she had been to the manner born.

Early mornings with Gertie learning about how this big place worked. Always dressed by 10:00, she and Miss Emma began a series of "young lady enrichment" exercises that included needlepoint, reading of poetry, serving of tea, and the arrangement of flowers.

Surprisingly, Jessie loved it. She loved the attention, all of the newness, all the feeling of being special. Oh, sometimes Gertie would find her under the staircase on the back porch of the house crying for her mother. Gertie first tried to reassure her herself, but soon found the person who could really pick her up out of this sadness was the master of the house, Douglas Strickland.

He bought her a pig one time and, while building a pen for it, started a series of events that would bring a whole slew of animals to this elaborate but cold mansion. To follow were three cats, two dogs, a horse and a very pregnant bunny that soon had the house literally jumping with bunnies.

As the years rolled by, Jessie grew into the child that the Stricklands always wanted. Douglas was always careful to protect this young, spirited child from Emma's more stringent demands, fearing that "too much tug on a young animal's mouth can break their spirit."

Less and less he would look at that locket in the desk drawer and finally in 1917, five years after Jessie had come into his life, he brought the locket to Jessie and gave it to her as a gift. Jessie recognized it to be the locket from her dad's desk, the one that belonged to Mr. Strickland's mother. She opened the locket and there was a picture of her herself that had been taken in Staunton at Blakemore's Studio. She thanked him and then threw her arms around his neck.

"You have made the need to keep that locket go away, Jessie. The picture that has been there for so long was of my sister Emily, my twin sister. You and she look so much alike and you are so much like her," he said as he raised his hands to his face. Not wanting to have to cry in front of Jessie, he excused himself and went outside on the front porch. There, leaning against one of the huge white columns, Douglas began to cry.

Jessie took the locket and ran to the garden where Gertie and Jeremy were hoeing weeds. Opening the gate, Jessie ran to Gertie and showed her what she had received. "Well, that be purty, Miss Jessie. Real purty." Gertie said. Taking Gertie by the hand, Jessie led her to the end of the row she was hoeing. "Gertie, Dad Strickland started to cry when he gave this to me and he said the picture that was in it was of his sister. Why did he get so upset Gertie? I don't understand."

Gertie was, that day, and would continue to be little Jessie's "real momma." So taking her out of the garden and out of Jeremy's earshot, she told the little girl how that Mr. Strickland's sister had fallen from a hayloft shortly after that locket picture had been taken and that she was never "quite right" after that.

Jessie still didn't understand and asked again why Dad Strickland was so upset. "Well, you see, Mr. Strickland felt that he was responsible for what happened to her that day and until you came along he could not forgive himself. But I will tell you this Jessie, since you been here, child, Mr. Strickland has been happier than I have ever seen him. It's the truth."

It would be that way for seven years. From 1912 to 1919, Jessie would grow and learn and expand her horizons as the much-loved foster daughter of Emma and Douglas Strickland. As she grew, she continued to show that spirit that Douglas loved to see. Oh, sometimes it led to such things as getting cow shards on a "Sunday-go-to-meeting" dress, riding her horse, Salem, under the clothes line, and dragging clean clothes from "here to damnation", as Gertie would say. And, there were nights when the Andes and Sutton girls would stop by and they would sneak off into the woods and smoke cigarettes. When she would be caught at such things, Miss Emma would "lay down the law" to Jessie and Jessie would cry. Douglas couldn't stand that and would always say, "Emma, don't be so hard on the girl. She's high spirited and after all, she really didn't do all that bad." He would then suggest that they all ride to Staunton, have a sundae at Hagwood's, go to the park and maybe the two women could go up to that milliners shop next to Col. Gardner's house and each get a new hat.

Jessie grew into a beautiful young woman before the Stricklands' eyes and it was with a great deal of trepidation that they called her into the living room that hot August day in 1919 to announce that because Dad Strickland needed to be located close to his growing home build-ing business in Staunton, that they were selling the house in Verona and moving there.

The first words out of Jessie's mouth were, "Please, no mother, this is my home. This is where all my friends are. Do we have to go, Mother?"

Douglas tried to explain to Jessie that Staunton was a better place to live. Good Schools, churches, stores, even a new theater was there. Jessie was not impressed. But, having visited the new house on the corner of Coalter St. and Kalorama St., and being told she could have her friends come to visit, and that she could decorate her own room, stable her horse, Salem, at Mr. Nelson's barn behind the Nutt's house up on Beverley St., she began to warm to the idea. Knowing that Gertie would be going with them also softened the blow.

Thus, on September 3rd 1919, Douglas and Emma Strickland, Miss Jessie, Gertie and as big an assortment of animals that the Strickland's could load into two cars and two trucks, left the mansion in Verona and moved to Staunton.

If they knew what was to happen to Jessie in the summer of 1922, Douglas would later say, "I would never have moved and furthermore, I would have tied Jessie down and watched her 24 hours a day."

Douglas Strickland would go on to be a prominent businessman in Staunton, Virginia and in hindsight, would continue to duplicate the freestanding staircase that he had first built when he renovated the mansion in Verona. Finishing up the staircase in McArthur Paine's home, Douglas took Emma and Jessie to see it. Jessie ran up the newly built stairs and descending them said, "Oh dad, it's just like the big house in Verona." Time had passed but the young girl with the locket descending the stairs made all the work worthwhile.

7

"Dinner at the Strickland's"

"When a person who has grown up poor meets cultured, well bred folks, the poorer person always seems to be at a loss for words." My father would write these words on a small pad of paper that I discovered in the desk in his bedroom. There among other yellow, faded pages were other words of perspective written by my father, as he was bedridden in the days before his death.

These words were proven to be true for him many times in his personal and professional life but never more than that cold dark evening of November 19th, 1922. That night, my father had been invited to the big house on Kalorama St. for dinner with the Stricklands. As the day approached, the reward dinner for having saved Mr. Strickland's life, hung as some kind of Damocles sword over his head.

Over and over again he tried to recall how the dining rooms on those Gospel Hill houses were laid out. He had seen them as he had delivered various purchases to the matrons of those homes. They had seemed so grand with their tear-dropped chandeliers and raised paneled cherry sideboards. The thickness of the marble tops on the tables had been amazing to him. Once in the beautiful Holt's house on the corner of Beverley and Coalter Street he had actually seen a dining table "turned out" with the extra leaves of the table put in place, covered with the most vividly white, embroidered linen tablecloth that hung almost to the floor. In the light from the eight-armed chandelier he had seen hand folded linen napkins atop gold edged china with the napkins formed in an angel wing fashion. He had seen all of the beautiful silverware with three or four forks, two or three knives, individual saltcellars, and finger bowls of water at each place setting.

"Luther, let's be going!!!" he could hear Shorty Minter say as he stood there that day in the Holts' house. "The Holts will be back soon and Mr. Davis is gonna wonder why it took us so long to deliver that table." The words entered into Luther's mind but he remained transfixed by what he saw and then it hit him. "I don't know what all those knives and forks are for!"

Two days to go before his dinner at the Strickland's and he was no better prepared to go than when it had been offered to him that day at the store. Why had he said yes? "Don't they already think I'm a clod?" He shook his head as he looked out on this wonderful dinner setting and could only foresee a giant catastrophe in the making. "Those people have special training Luther, in all those "hoity-toity" ways and we don't" he could hear his mother say. "Luther, that Joyce Simmons girl would be a good catch for you. She's a big girl and a hard worker. She's got a good job over at the laundry at Western State Hospital. I've seen her looking at you at church and your daddy knows her daddy from down at the gas plant."

As he prepared to go to bed on Saturday night, and with less than 24 hours before the dinner, Luther was a nervous wreck. What would he talk about? What stupid mistake would he make? Why had he been so excited about going? If it were just Jessie, he felt he could handle it. He had talked to lots of rich girls before in the store and had not been intimidated by them. As a matter of fact, Mr. Davis seemed really sort of put off by the time some of these "daughter's of Staunton's finest" had spent at his counter as Luther waited on them. Finally, he drifted off into a fitful sleep.

Sunday broke cold and damp as Luther rose early to tend the coal stove in the kitchen/living room of the Brown's cold-water row house. The mismatched pieces of rug covering the floor; leftovers from jobs that the Banner store had sold, could not keep the cold wind from entering the cracks in the floor so Luther, in his stocking covered feet, sort of crow-hopped around as he stoked the "almost out" stove. He blew on his hands and noticed how the cold outside wind had scored the broken kitchen window with ice crystals. Luther had lain in his comforter-covered bed as long as he could, but the air coming through the bedroom grate in his room told him the stove was almost out and needed tending.

As he looked around his poor surroundings, he so wished that he were somewhere else, was someone else, in a world that he knew and understood.

Church was a family affair for the Browns so the weekly walk up Kalorama Street out to the Baptist Church on West Beverley Street was a common sight. Except on this Sunday, Luther would request that "Today let's go a different way to church." To his surprise, no one disagreed. So this Irish clan of mother, father, four boys and two girls could be seen this Sunday cutting up the alley beside the Nelson's stable and the Nutt's family home up to Beverley Street and down that main street past the clock tower to church.

Whatever Rev. Dunsmore preached on that Sunday, Luther could not recall, lost as he was in his own thoughts. He had left his new shirt, new collar, polished black shoes and best pants and coat at his Aunt Vivian's house on Hampton Street with the plan being that he would excuse himself right after lunch, saying he had to meet George Gibson, his cousin, at George's house.

After church, Luther hurried through lunch and, kissing his mother on the cheek, he said he would be back in a little while. Mothers always seem to know when something is going on in the life of one of their own and, grabbing her son's arm, she said, "Everything alright Luther? You didn't hardly touch your food." Luther said he was fine and quickly left the house and made for Sears Hill and Hampton Street.

George Gibson, Luther's cousin, was pretty much the chosen one in the Gibson family. Bright and thoughtful, Luther often times confided in him and what he wanted to do with his life.

George was one relative that was always positive and had the distinct quality of being able to keep a secret.

The two boys hurried to George's room where George had ironed and then laid out Luther's "dinner outfit." The two boys talked excitedly about the approaching event and the great possibility it held. George related how he too had a relationship with one of Staunton's finest, Elizabeth Cochran, and how nervous he had been and how things had worked out well.

The young men spent the afternoon talking and at about four o'clock Luther took a bath in the Gibson's full sized bathtub, shaved, doused on some of his recently purchased lilac water, and dressed himself.

In the hallway of the Gibson house was a long mirror on the front of a huge wardrobe. Luther stopped there and looked at himself in the mirror. Not too bad, he thought. Maybe a little skinny, but all right.

As he turned to go, his Aunt Vivian stopped him at the door and, kissing his cheek, pressed a fresh white linen handkerchief into his hand. "All gentlemen have to have a fresh handkerchief when they go out, darling," she said.

Later, when he opened it, there was a freshly picked four-leaf clover in the handkerchief for luck for her Irish nephew.

Approaching the Strickland house, Luther could feel this terrible knot in his stomach. For a moment he thought he was going to be sick, but at that instant he looked up and there on the porch, straight across the street, was Mr. Strickland. Gold tipped, straight cherry cane in his hand, small pinch nez glasses balanced on his nose. Dad would later say he looked exactly like Teddy Roosevelt!

He crossed the street, walked up to the porch and into the firmest handshake he had ever encountered. Luther looked straight into one of the most kind and happy faces he had ever seen. Luther had no experience with this. Most of his previous experiences with the wealthy and well bred of Staunton had been that they were cold and distant, very conscious of their position and quick to judge.

None of this emanated from Mr. Douglas Strickland. Later Dad would learn that Doug Strickland came from the poor side of the Strickland family, had worked his way through college and had done every job he had ever asked one of his employees to do.

As he held Dad's hand, he seemed like a genuinely good person and Dad could feel some of his initial apprehension drain away. It was replaced by an awareness that this person in front of him was a man of some depth and purpose. As the architect/builder talked and the Banner store clerk listened, Luther could tell that this older man had done some homework as far as he was concerned. He knew who his father was, knew his assorted uncles and aunts, and what kind of young man had pulled him from that burning truck. What he did not talk about however was anything that had to do with Jessie and that, in the final analysis, would be the real test.

After what seemed an eternity, but probably not more than five minutes, Mr. Strickland led Luther into the house and turned left into the living room with it's coal burning fireplace. It immediately struck Luther that this room was bigger than the whole downstairs of his home.

As the two men passed through the living room into the dining room, Luther could see his image in the six foot long gold leafed mirror that rested above the dining room sideboard cabinet. His hair, blown by the wind, stood straight up on the back of his head like an out of control cowlick. Instinctively, he spat on his fingers and found the errant hairs just as Mrs. Strickland came into the room.

Doggone it!! He thought. Here I am trying to make a good impression on these folks and she catches me spitting on my head.

Mrs. Strickland pretended not to see all this and extended her elegant hand in welcome. Luther nervously extended his own right hand, the one he had used to doctor his hair, and immediately caught the difference in the warm handshake of Mr. Strickland and this one from Mrs. Strickland. Cold, insincere and not at all welcoming or reassuring, her cold penetrating eyes showed the breeding of four generations of Virginia wealth.

All of these feelings passed quickly as, into the room walked the most beautiful woman Luther had ever seen. She smiled at my father and extended her hand and my father would later say, "The world stopped, his breath stopped and although he could see her lips moving, his hearing stopped as well." She must have asked a question because she looked like someone who expected a response. Dad said something like "How do you do" or something equally enchanting. He said he was transfixed. He couldn't move and couldn't think. He was scared to death.

The terrible crashing of a silver platter brought all those in the room, back to reality. "Gracie" shouted Mrs. Strickland, "What in the world are you doing now?" The cook/servant, Gracie, bent down low and picked up the heaving tray from the tiled butler's pantry floor and replied "Nuthin, Mrs. Emma, nuthin." With that, she quickly left the room.

"Won't you come into the parlor Mr. Brown?" Mrs. Strickland said and pointing with those long fingers of hers, directed the four into the front room.

The room was dark, Luther thought, with wine-colored drapes hanging heavy with their gold tassels on the windows. The furniture was period cherry and walnut and nicely covered with doilies on all the armrests. The dark carpets added to the quietness of the room with brass gaslights on the sidewalls providing the light.

Mr. Strickland got up from his chair and crossed the room to prod the coal fire back to life. Luther sat down on a high-backed sofa while Jessie and Mrs. Emma sat on a Victorian loveseat covered in red velvet.

All these things my father remembered years later as we would sit in the garden on wooden apple crates and he would drink water I had brought him from the bucket on the porch.

Mrs. Strickland asked, "Mr. Brown, are you related to the Macon Browns who have the big apple orchard out at Folly Mills?" The interrogation had begun. Seeking to keep the conversation on what he was rather than who he was, Mr. Strickland interjected that Luther's father worked at the gas plant and he and his family originally had a farm up in Newport, VA. Luther was surprised by this act of kindness from Mr.

Strickland but later, would learn that he, Mr. Strickland, had encountered such an interrogation from Emma's father the first time he visited her father's house.

The conversation ran around the room rather graciously after that and Luther was slowly gaining his footing as he responded to questions about what were the newest home decorating trends, the quality of the new Venetian blinds that had just arrived at the store and how that some of the new chintz materials were really beautiful. All of this came to an end when Gracie entered the room to announce that dinner was served.

Moving up to the table, with Mr. Strickland at the head at one end and Mrs. Emma at the other, Luther grabbed the back of his chair to sit down on the side facing Miss Jessie. It was then he realized that Jessie was looking at him from across the table. It hit him like a lightning bolt, "real gentlemen will pull out the chair and seat the lady when at a proper dinner situation."

Quickly, he went around the table and pulled out Jessie's chair and instinctively placed his hand on her back to assist her in seating herself. He did not know if he had done the right thing or not but he felt that he had. This was all so new to him.

Upon sitting down, he noticed Gracie going around the table removing and then placing the table napkin on each person's lap.

"Let us say a few words of blessing before our meal," Mr. Strickland said as he bowed his head. Luther was a Baptist and as such, had no creeds or blessings at his table. He also bowed his head, but not before looking up and seeing Jessie looking right at him and smiling as she too bowed her head.

The meal went well with no real problems thanks mostly to the etiquette crash course his Aunt Vivian had provided. Aunt Vivian had two years of college at the Staunton Women's Preparatory School due to a gift from a wealthy patron of her church. She had learned all the social ins and outs about needlepoint and French conversation. Lost now in her Gibson house with her blacksmith husband and four Irish boys, she had really seemed excited to tell Dad which fork to use with which course, how and when to use the finger bowls and the individual saltcellars. The food was delicious and the dessert pudding to die for. Mr. Strickland rose after the dessert and said to Dad, "Son, I want to talk to you alone for a while, so ladies, if you will excuse us for a moment?"

Dad followed Mr. Strickland into his office in the front left room of the house. Huge easels held drawings of houses and buildings. A black and white drawing of a freestanding staircase with a curved handrail stood on it's own in the corner of the room. A huge oak roll-top desk stood along one wall and Mr. Strickland approached it, picked up something and, returning to where Dad was standing, offered my Dad a cigar. Dad was a Baptist; no smoking, no drinking, and no dancing. Though his family enjoyed all three, Dad did not.

He took the offered cigar and followed Mr. Strickland over to the front window where two rocking chairs sat.

Sitting down, Mr. Strickland began speaking about when he started his business and how Staunton had changed so. He spoke of houses built and people met and how lumber had to air dry just so and how hard it was to get people to work these days.

My Dad felt that he was being the male stand-in for the son that Douglas never had and so he listened, hoping the fact that he had not lit his cigar would not come up.

Mr. Strickland must have talked on for at least twenty minutes without taking a breath, just looking out that front window and reminiscing about this and that. "BRINNNNNG" the high pitched ring of the gold watch in Douglas's pocket broke the quiet of the one man dialogue and removing his watch from his vest pocket and turning it off, he looked over at dad. Seeming a little embarrassed, he apologized for "going on so."

With that, the older man returned to his desk, picked up an envelope and offered it to Luther. "I want you to take this, it's really just a small token for your having saved my life the other night."

"No sir, I can't take that," my father said, all the while wondering how much it was and knowing how much it could help him financially. "I did not do what I did to get paid for it. I did it because it was the right thing to do."

"Well, maybe so son, but it still was a brave thing to do and you deserve to be paid for it." Mr. Strickland thrust the envelope at him again and said, "Take it son, don't' you know that money doesn't grow on trees and you probably could use it for you and your family?"

That hit a little too close to the bone for my father and he responded, "We do alright sir and we don't need your handout. I guess you don't understand who we are, living up here in this big house on the hill while we're down the street in the poor section, but we do all right for ourselves. All my brothers work and dad has a good job and we do just fine." The redness on his hot Irish neck could have burnt the celluloid collar right then and there. Oh Lord, open mouth and insert foot, my father thought now standing with chest out, reacting in a typical Irish tantrum. "Good Lord Luther, you came up here to make a good first impression and look at this mess you've caused."

Mr. Strickland looked at the visibly upset young man and using the grace that comes with age, he turned and placed the envelope back on his desk and said something to my father that he would never forget: "I'm sorry son, I didn't mean to make you mad with what I said. I was just trying to do what I thought was right. But I do thank you for what you did and maybe we will see more of each other in the future." He stuck his hand out to my father. My father transferred the unlit cigar from his right to his left hand and, feeling really sorry for what he had said, was led out into the hall and to the front door.

My father could see Jessie and Mrs. Strickland sitting in the gas-lit parlor, one doing needlepoint, the other reading a book. Neither looked up and he was sure they had heard his outburst. In later years, my father would say that was the longest two-mile walk he ever took that night; over to Hampton St. for his clothes and back home by way of the Lewis Creek footbridge.

As he laid there on the bed that night listening to his brother's night sounds, he felt he had really blown it and that surely that pretty girl on top of the hill would never speak to him again.

8

"The Die is Cast"

The morning after the dinner, Jessie did not come down to breakfast, as was her usual custom. The events of the night before continued to play out in her mind and with each playing, she felt worse about what had happened.

She knew that Mrs. Emma would feel vindicated as Luther's response to the gift showed his "lack of breeding." Jessie knew that when she did go downstairs that her foster mother would want to use the evening as a proof that one needs to stay in her own social caste.

At about 9:30, Jessie came downstairs to find Mrs. Emma sitting in the parlor waiting for her. In instinctive fashion, the older woman pulled the gold watch chain down from its' shoulder pin, glanced at it and without saying a word let Jessie know that the young woman was starting the day off by being late.

"Come in here dear, it's too late for breakfast but I'll have Gracie bring us some tea and muffins." With that she rang her ever-present bell and Gracie scurried in. "Gracie, bring us some tea and those fresh muffins you made yesterday. Jessie and I will take them on the front porch."

With that, this elegant southern lady extended her arm and Jessie respectfully helped her out of her chair.

Once the two women reached the porch, the lesson began. "Jessie," Emma said, "I hope the events of last evening have helped you see why Douglas and I have tried to school you in proper etiquette and behavior. There are certain rules and expectations that a young girl needs to know and we have worked hard to teach you these responses and duties."

Jessie could hear Mrs. Emma's words. She could see her mouth moving and her hands pointing to emphasize some point or other, but Jessie was not at all interested in what she was saying. She would sit there on that big porch, ankles crossed demurely, one hand covering the other, all in the world looking like the ever-attentive, disciplined young thing that Mrs. Emma had worked so hard to create.

Jessie appreciated all that the Stricklands had done or had tried to do but under the surface, there still was this other person trying to get out. For Jessie, with all the societal trappings, was still the product of an unwed country mother's love affair with a man that Jessie had never seen. Even with all that had been done to raise her "in the right way", there were dark corners of her memory that recalled harsh voices, angry threats and always, always this vision of a young woman running down a farm lane crying at a model T and stopping at a bridge with one hand across her face and the other hand reaching out to the vanishing car.

Because of all the close maintenance Emma had placed on her, Jessie really lived in two worlds. The one, ordered and controlled, belonged to the Stricklands. The other, which was requiring more and more time to control as she grew older, was a wilder, freer, out-of-control world where she envisioned one could do anything one wanted with few constraints.

It was into this second world that Luther Ardley Brown had unknowingly entered that first day she had seen him. Slim, muscular, dark, athletic, severe: he represented that long suppressed world she dreamed of living in. A world of adventure, of excitement and most importantly, of love.

"You do understand what I'm saying, don't you dear?" Emma said as she tapped Jessie on her folded hands. "What? Yes. Yes mam," Jessie sputtered, having just been brought back into her first world.

Jessie smiled, Emma smiled, and the lesson was finished, at least as far as Emma was concerned. As Jessie ate her muffin, Mrs. Emma seemed pleased with the way the morning had gone.

What Jessie really wanted to say to her was that they shouldn't have tried to give Luther any thing. Hadn't he said in the store that he didn't need to be paid for doing the right thing? She thought that, but she said nothing. Arguing protocol or behavior with Mrs. Emma would lead to naught, so she thought her own private thoughts, ate her muffin, drank her tea and planned how she would see him again, regardless of what anyone said.

Patterns of behavior in a small southern town are quite predictable and in a society where everyone knows what everyone else is doing, it did not take Jessie long to figure out ways to "bump into" Luther while making it look innocent and by chance.

From Brenda Minter she learned that Luther often times spent Sundays in the park and also loved the carousel rides in the amusement area out on Churchville Avenue.

So it was that Jessie May Rohr, the foster child of Emma and Douglas Strickland, aged 17 going on 25, who had set her bonnet for Luther Ardley Brown, aged 23, began a series of chance encounters to catch him.

My mother in later years would admit she did not realize how danger-ous a path she had chosen, nor how many lives she would affect with her actions. She was young, she was headstrong, and she was commit-ted to live her life her way and the "Devil take the hindmost."

Their initial rendezvous were quite innocent, quite public, but if she was expecting this older Irish boy from down the hill to restrain her, she had badly miscalculated. With every soda, every trolley ride, every cotton candy shared in the park, he became more certain of this uncer-tain course they had set out upon.

Now came the overnights to girlfriends and the evening meetings as this whirlwind of an affair gained speed. First kiss, first promises, gave away to talk of marriage, of children and of a life together.

Both agreed that a "real family" had to have several children and that the real reason people were put on this earth was to grow up, get mar-ried, have children, and to grow old as a married couple.

These kinds of dialogues went on effortlessly as these two different, yet very similar people walked, talked and fell hopelessly in love. Dad would later say that these "chance meetings" had taken all of his God-given good sense away and as he would return home his feet did not seem to touch the pavement.

How they kept their secret in that little southern, gossipy town remains a mystery. Probably the best explanation ever put forward was given by my aunt Helen Ramsey (actually a second cousin, but older and called "Aunt Helen") who said that probably the reason that the eleven-month adventure had gone on without "anyone important being the wiser," was that Mr. Strickland was so respected and loved Jessie so openly that no one who saw Luther and Jessie together would want to be the one carrying the bad news. Also, people knew what Luther had done that night to save Douglas' life and that, like Luther, Douglas had come from a working family background and had probably encountered some of that "high, Strickland family nose in the air" attitude himself. And certainly no one was going to tell Mrs. Emma that her well thought out plans of a spring wedding to one of Staunton's finest was going to be derailed.

Jessie would, for her part, have just enough dates, chaperoned and quite proper, to keep down the suspicions. She would stand at her front gate and speak of this and that to Thomas Hagwood, the pharmacist's son, and to Charlie Moffet when he would ride his handsome horse up Kalorama Street hill from Mr. Nelson's barn. She would accompany her foster mother to various social teas and go as an invited guest to socials and dances given by the blue bloods of Gospel Hill.

All of this subterfuge, romance, and excitement could have continued except an event would occur that would change everything: Thomas Hagwood became 23!

His father had sent him to the "very proper" University of Virginia, to pharmacy school at the University of Richmond and now, Dr. Thomas Hagwood was home in Staunton and beginning his practice as a pharmacist in his father's drug store. Even though his mother had Emma Strickland's dreams for her son, it had been obvious for a long time that the only woman of young Tom's dreams was Jessie, that beautiful young girl that had moved in to Dr. Harmon's old house four years before and who had totally captured his heart. As vivacious as she was, he was nervous around people, as neat and trim as she was, he always looked, as he would say, "Like he just fell out of a hearse". His big feet were always in the way, he lacked any kind of athletic grace and at any period that you would view in his life, he always seemed like he was growing out of his clothes.

The harder his mother had pushed, the more Thomas had resisted, but now he was back in Staunton, unmarried and quite available.

If her son could not marry well on his own, his mother decided she would help him along. So began a long line of young ladies from good families that found their way into Hagwood's Drug Store ostensibly to purchase this medicinal powder or other but what were really intended as created opportunities for Tom to meet the finest young ladies that Staunton had to offer.

Tommy Hagwood was no better at handling these situations than those his mother had contrived while he was at UVA. Finally, after hearing the "Thomas you have so much to offer and you know how your father would love to have grand-children" speech, Tommy blurted out, in frustration as much as anything, "Mother, please, I don't care about any of these girls, I just don't, but if I did want to get married to someone, I wouldn't have to go out of the neighborhood to find her. I'd choose Jessie!" And with that, he left the table.

Mrs. Hagwood had been a Timberlake before she had married Thomas's father. Her mother had been from the Richard Bell family, an original colonizer of the Shenandoah Valley. Her view of the girl that she wanted for her son was as cloaked in bloodline as it was in the personality of the chosen girl.

The outburst from her always quiet, always shy, son resulted in Anna Bell Timberlake Hagwood's whole world tilting slightly askew.

The wind was out of her sails. Her carefully scripted plans thrown to the wind. "Jessie Rohr," she thought, "She isn't even the Strickland's real child!!"

For a week after Thomas's outburst at the dinner table Anna Hagwood looked at putting a good spin on what had happened to her plans for her only son. After an afternoon tea at the Holt's house she began to reconsider a little bit. For at the tea, sitting in the Holt's beautiful front room, was no one else but Mrs. Emma Strickland herself and that girl, Jessie. After an appropriate period of tea and womanly discussion with Mrs. Holt, and Mrs. Gibbs and Mrs. Nutt, wealthy women all, all having sons recently married, she saw that Jessie had gotten up from her table and gone out on the street side porch for a breath of fresh air. Mrs. Hagwood saw this as her chance to close the distance with this young lady, as she would later tell her oldest friends, "To take measure of her as a woman."

Approaching this beautiful auburn haired young woman, it was all that she could do not to push her off that high porch. Maybe she would fall down on the trolley tracks and get run over!!

Placing her scented handkerchief under her nose and coughing was Anna's way of breaking the silence between her and this young girl that Mrs. Hagwood had oftentimes seen, but had never considered as a suitable wife for her Thomas.

"Achoo!" she said, afraid her sneezing theatrics might have been too much.

Jessie turned. At seventeen years of age Jessie was a beautiful woman and well schooled in the social arts of repartee. "Bless you, Mrs. Hagwood," she said with not one slight hint of loss of station. "It seems that a lot of people have come down with a cough or cold these last few days," she said.

She was not supposed to be so pretty, Anna thought. She seems so nice. She doesn't even seem intimidated by me, as I would have been when I met my husband's mother.

The two women entered into conversation, the one measuring and analyzing every word and the other speaking lightly and happily. Anna thought, "This young girl carries herself very well. Mrs. Strickland has done a good job."

But what would turn this chance meeting into a real happening occurred when my mother started talking about Anna's son Thomas; about what a good young man he was and how she had enjoyed getting to know him, how she had danced with him at the Staunton Young Ladies Club dance at the pavilion at the park, how he was doing such a good job at her husband's store. "Oh I put it on pretty thick", my mother would recall later. "I would have done anything to get that beady-eyed little woman away from me. You could tell by the way she treated me that she was just sizing me up and I made my mind up that day that, although I wouldn't raise my voice like Luther had to Douglas Strickland, I would not stand there and let this woman continue to look me up and down as if I was somehow suspect because I did not share her or the Strickland's bloodline."

She had seen it before when other persons of station, who, having heard she was not the "real" child of the Strickland's, had changed in the way they treated her.

Maybe she was overreacting but by being vibrant and forthcoming, she had inadvertently set her destiny in motion.

Following the tea, and for weeks after, Mrs. Hagwood used every opportunity to "bump into" Jessie and Emma Strickland. At the Second Presbyterian Church, at the ladies' luncheon, at the garden club meeting, at the Confederate Daughter's workday at the Thornrose cemetery. Any opportunity was created or contrived. After this series of events, Anna was ready.

She told her husband of her recent discoveries about the Stricklands and their very desirable young ward and that she thought she would have a discussion with Mrs. Emma about her plans for Jessie. Dr. Hagwood was aghast. "What's wrong with you woman? We have known the Stricklands and their families for years. Little Jessie has been coming into my store since she was five or six years old. Way back when they used to live at the big white house down in Verona, before he bought Dr. Harmon's house down the street." Pointing to the front hall, he said, "Douglas Strickland built that landing out there in that hallway as a special favor for me because we are both Masons. Anna, you just can't go down there and ask them what their plans are for their foster child, you just can't."

Anna was used to this response to any of her suggestions, but she knew what needed to be done and she selected the night of August 3, a Tuesday, to go talk to Emma Strickland. She would have Hannah bake some cookies. She would dream up some pretense to visit and then she would "sort Emma out", as to what her intentions were for her child, Jessie.

This visit would be planned for Tuesday night because that was the night the Masons always met and both her husband and Douglas Strickland would be gone. If the meeting went badly, her husband would never know. Little did Anna Hagwood know what that innocent meeting would do to the lives of so many.

9

"Two for the Road"

My mother would learn of the Hagwood visit to Emma Strickland when she returned from Verona where she had been visiting her childhood friends: the Andes girls and the Sutton family with their six children. She had fished and swam in Middle River down below the mill, had ridden her horse Salem that the Suttons were now keeping for her and generally had a great time with people she always had loved. She took one afternoon to clean off the headstone of Gertie, the gentle old black nanny that had been her first "real mother" when young Jessie first came to live with the Stricklands. Gertie had died only four weeks after moving to Staunton and mother was just now getting over it. She had asked Helen and May Andes to drive her over to the "colored people's" cemetery and then, after she had cleaned off the stone and put the wild flowers on the grave, she asked the other girls if they could just go on back to the car so that she could have a little "private time" with Gertie.

"Gertie, I miss you so," young Jessie said as she knelt in front of Gertie's grave. "I see you everywhere I go and miss your kindness and your wisdom. Gertie, I have come today to tell you some news that I just gotta tell someone or I'm gonna pop. Gertie, I have found him. You know how you used to talk about your husband Hiram, and how when you were young that he had been the "moon and stars" of your life? Well, that's how I feel about Luther. He doesn't have much money, Gertie, but he's got a good job and he pulled Dad Strickland out of his wrecked truck and everybody says he is a real hero. Mom Strickland doesn't like him and is pushin that Hagwood boy at me but, I really do love Luther and when I'm with him Gertie, I feel so excited and warm and all."

"Jessie, are you all right?" Helen Andes yelled down from the parked car at the road. She could hear Jessie talking to Gertie's grave and worried about her easily excitable friend.

"I'm all right, Helen. I'll just be another minute or so." Jessie now realized she had been talking out loud and so she slid closer to Gertie's headstone to continue her conversation.

"Gertie, I need to tell you what I'm gonna do, actually what Luther and I are going to do. We have planned it all out and nobody can stop us. Mother Strickland has just about put her foot down about me and Luther seeing each other so, we have been sneaking around and bumping into each other here and there. But Gertie, I love him so and you and I know that I was never cut out for all this formal and genteel stuff that I've been taught. Gertie, I know who I am and I feel so comfortable with my Luther."
"Jessie, are you coming?" One of the girls had yelled at her. "In a minute, just a minute." Jessie said, waving her hand to keep her friends away.

"What we have decided to do is run off and get married and then the Stricklands will have to accept him. And if they don't, we will just get along fine without them. I have saved up almost sixty dollars and Luther has a bank account at the Valley National Bank. We are going to be just fine and I wanted you to know that I'm just following the advice you gave me when you said sometimes you just gotta follow your heart. I have to go Gertie." Jessie said as she rose from the gravesite. "Wish me luck and I'll come back to tell you how it all worked out." And with that, the young Jessie turned and ran to the car where her nervous friends were waiting. Before the night was through, Jessie would relate to the girls what their role would be in her plans. She would tell them she had already laid a trousseau out for herself and it would be tucked into her suitcase that she would be carrying to Verona on her next visit. The plan would be that she would tell Mother Strickland that she wanted to go to the "Sham Battle" at the Augusta Military School on Saturday the 18th of August, two weeks hence and that once in Verona, the girls would drive her over to the Fort Defiance railway station where Luther and she would meet up, catch the train to Hyattsville, Maryland and get married.

The girls, sitting on the beds in the Andes' girl's bedroom, started to scream, "Oh Jessie! It's just like Romeo and Juliet!" they gushed. All night amongst twitters and covered mouth excitement, the girls agreed to be a part of this wonderful scheme.

Where they would live, how they would live, and what would the Stricklands' response be? None of these questions were ever discussed. My mother would later say that no two people had been less prepared for marriage and yet totally innocent in their love. The reality would be something like Scarlet O'Hara might say, "To be worried about another day."

As the days drew down to the planned weekend, signs continued to appear that told the two star-crossed lovers that their plan was sound and as my mother would say, "Destined to be."

First, Dad Strickland and Mother Strickland announced at the dinner table one night how that there was to be a Masonic Lodge National Meeting in Richmond and how they were making plans to attend. The date—August 18th! It was like a sign from heaven for Jessie and she responded that the Andes family had invited her down to Verona for the Civil War Sham Battle recreation on that weekend and she so wanted to go. Jessie had gone to these Civil War affairs before and Emma, being a flag-carrying Daughter of the Confederacy member had always encouraged Jessie to go.

So, that was settled. Mom and Dad Strickland out of town, the Andes' girls in agreement and now, the time had come.

If the plans for the proposed wedding had gone "smooth as silk" for Jessie, the groom would later say that those two weeks before the event were like a living hell that would so shake him that it would be almost 30 years before he would tell Jessie how he had felt as the chosen day approached.

Luther Brown had never been over 90 miles from Staunton in all his life and that had been in a Banner Store truck with Shorty Minter and Bob Sprouse when they went, three across in a seat, to Roanoke to pick up the first Venetian blind machine that Staunton had ever seen.

In these two weeks before the event, this non-traveler had to find out where you could go to get married on the "quick and easy", how much it cost, and how they would get there. What or what not to tell his parents? What if the Stricklands got "up in the air" about the marriage? Was he even sure that he wanted to get married? All of these questions and more came at Luther who was a person who, above all else, lived his whole life with his shoes lined up, who always made "a to-do list", and had this real need to know what he was to do and in what order it was to be done.

When he and Jessie had discussed these runaway-to-get-married ideas, it seemed to be doable but with so many "what ifs" out there, every day seemed worse than the next.

On his little lined pad that he always carried in his coat pocket, he wrote the items down one by one. From his only confidant, his Aunt Vivian, he learned that Hyattsville, Maryland was the place to go to get married if you didn't want to have too many questions asked and you wanted to be married in a hurry.

From a chance meeting with Harry Ralston, the town clerk, he had learned that, at least in Virginia, the cost of a marriage license was three dollars. He received that information after having taken one of Harry's "Ralston for Clerk" political buttons, promising to vote for Harry come November, and after quizzing Harry about other licenses that Harry was responsible for, including the license fee for keeping a hog in the city limits, the cost of business license and how long did you have to wait for a birth certificate from Richmond if a person wanted such a thing.

After visiting the Staunton train station, Luther got a train schedule that included all the stops and the times of these stops of the Chesapeake and Ohio passenger trains that could take him to Hyattsville, Maryland

Luther got his trousseau together, borrowed his cousin George's suitcase, stored them for the time being over at his cousin's house, withdrew the handsome sum of $108.50 from his growing account at the Valley National Bank and purchased, for seventy-five cents, a one-way ticket from Staunton to the Fort Defiance train station, that according to Mr. Landrum, the station manager, would stop at around 10:00 Saturday morning at Fort Defiance. All was ready and then he looked at the bottom of his list: tell your parents that you and your cousin George were going fishing Saturday out at the Ramsey's farm in Mint Spring. An additional matter of how he was to get out of working Saturday was going to be taken care of by coughing and sneezing all day Friday so that Mr. Davis could hear him and say, as he always did,

"Luther, you sound terrible son. If you are not better by tomorrow morning, stay home."

It had always worked before and although Luther knew that it wasn't totally Mr. Davis' interest in dad's health that would lead him to tell Luther to stay home, but rather, how would it appear to have a sick employee in his store. Bad business, you know.

There it was. All done. My father would later tell me that he must have lost five pounds in those two weeks before August 18th and that if he looked at and questioned those lines written in #2 pencil on that pad, one time, he must have looked at them a hundred times.

It has been said that God looks out for "fools and lovers" and certainly He must have been looking out for my mother and my father that weekend in August of 1923.

Mom got to the Andes' house and the girls got mom to the Ft. Defiance train station. Dad's excuses to parents and boss were accepted, and he got to the Ft. Defiance train station at exactly 10:00 a.m. Saturday morning. He purchased two tickets to Maryland with transfers to the town of Hyattsville, MD under the amused gaze of James Moyer, the station manager. "Hyattsville, huh?" Mr. Moyer said. "You two kids are not from around here are you?" My dad would later relate how he had never been so scared in his life and mom said she had never been so glad to have worn a large straw hat and was carrying a beautifully turned parasol, both of which helped to keep her face from Mr. Moyer's gaze.

The train took on water, the conductor called the passengers to the train, and two of the scaredest kids in Augusta County climbed aboard the first train that either of them had ever ridden.

Once seated, the two would sit almost motionless and say little as the train moved out from the station heading north.

Two transfers and five hours later, dad and mom stood before a magistrate in an old antebellum home. After perusing the newly acquired license and having collected $3.50 from my father, the magistrate said some words and my dad put the gold ring on my mother's finger that would stay there for the next seventy-four years.

Getting back to the "nice little boarding house" the magistrate had recommended, the newlyweds dropped off their two suitcases and went downtown in Hyattsville to eat supper. After a long walk, the two young people went back to the boarding house and then the trouble began.

Years later, my mother would say she didn't know what came over her that night but the idea of sleeping in the same bed with Luther Brown suddenly caused her to start to cry. And cry she did, off and on for almost four hours. By the time she finished, Luther had retreated to an upholstered chair across the room, kicked off his shoes, and out of exhaustion, fell asleep.

Mother would say that there she sat, in that beautiful walnut four-poster bed, her wedding suit, beautiful black broach at her neck, black hose and black patent leather high-button shoes on, and listened, between crying jags, to her husband's gentle breathing across the room.

The next morning, the two would have breakfast at the station, get back on the train and return to Staunton. Not more that one hundred words were exchanged in that five hour trip home but one question completely dominated both of their minds: "What have we done and what are we going to do now?"

10

"Children of Mine— Mother of Mine"

The steam rolling out of the bottom of the train distorted the view that Jessie and Luther Brown had of the passenger platform when their train finally pulled into Staunton. It was now Sunday, August 19th, and because of delays it was a little after 8:00 p.m. As they stepped from the train they had no idea what was getting ready to take place.

The telephone had rung in Douglas and Emma Strickland's room at 9:00 p.m. Saturday night. The Masonic meeting had broken up at about 7 and after a quick supper, the two were back at their room in the John Marshall Hotel. They had not been back long when the telephone rang.

"Hello Mr. Strickland, this is the desk manager from downstairs. There is a telephone call for you and your wife from someone in Verona, Virginia. They say they need to talk to you. Should I patch the call through to you, sir? Sir?"

A knot immediately formed in Douglas Strickland's stomach. "What could have happened that someone needs to talk to me? It's got to have something to do with Jessie," Douglas thought.

"Sir, about the call?"

"Yes, yes put them through," Douglas said as he looked around his hotel room to find the door to the bathroom was closed. Emma was out of earshot.

"Douglas, this is Tom Andes calling from Verona, Virginia. I have had a dickens of a time finding you." Douglas recognized the voice of Tom Andes. He had been a neighbor and a friend for all the years that he and Emma had lived in Verona. A good fellow, he thought and then asked, "Tom, is there something wrong. Is Jessie alright?"

"Well, that's what I've called you about. I hope you are not going to be mad at me and the missus but it seems we have been made part of some kind of conspiracy involving Jessie and some fellow named Brown."

Douglas heard the name Brown and his heart jumped into his throat as if he had been shot. "What? What are you talking about, Tom? Jessie is supposed to be staying the weekend with you and your wife. She's supposed to be going to the Sham Battle at the school down there."

"Well, Douglas, that's supposed to be what was to happen but it seems that this Brown fellow has gotten with Jessie and they both got on the train at Ft. Defiance headed north towards Maryland."

"Good God Man, how could such a thing happen?" Douglas asked with a voice so loud that Emma burst out of the bathroom shouting, "What's happened, Douglas? What's happened?"

Douglas held his hand up to his wife to stop her questions. She slapped his hand away from her face and said, "I said what happened and I want to know now!"

"It's Tom Andes on the phone mother. He says that Jessie has run off with that Brown boy to somewhere in Maryland." Emma backed up three steps, reaching for the arm of the chair. Instead, she knocked a bowl from the side chair's table. The bowl fell off of the table and crashed in a hundred pieces on the tiled vestibule floor.

"Oh no, how could this be? We have given her everything, treated her as our very own." She said as she sank heavily down into the chair and then pressed her face into her hands and started to cry.

Today it takes about an hour and a half to go from Richmond, Virginia to Staunton on Interstate 64. In 1923 it would take six to eight hours. Douglas Strickland was standing on the passenger platform at 6:00 a.m. on Sunday August 19th, 1923. How he and Emma got there is still a mystery, but they were there and so was Sam Shifflet, the chief of police of Staunton and two of his men.

From the station manager they found out that yes, a man and a young woman had purchased round trip tickets from Mr. Moyer at Ft. Defiance station and that the two were scheduled to be on the six o'clock train from Hyattsville, MD to Staunton.

During the train delay, Douglas kept Mr. Landrum busy on the railroad's telegraph checking the progress of the train and between trips back up Kalorama St. to tell Emma of the developments, he would go up to his workshop behind his house and try to think out what he was going to do. Every scenario he could think of ended badly. It was this state of mind that Douglas Strickland was in when he returned to the train station. He parked his car, and patting the bulged pocket of his thick long coat, made his way up to the passenger platform. Two uniformed policemen stood up when they saw him approach and one, a young officer named Cline, said, "The train's in Verona, Mr. Strickland. It will be here in about ten minutes." Douglas turned and looked down the curving track and could see the lights on the railroad bridge over Greenville Avenue come on. It was 8:00 p.m.

The first sign of trouble came when Luther stepped down off the train. He had turned to help Jessie down when he was grabbed by each arm by the policemen. Next, he saw Mr. Strickland coming toward him, coat open, and the walnut handle of a gun in his belt. Luther tried to pull away but Douglas's strong hand slapped him across the face with such force that my father went down. Douglas reached his hand up the train stairs for Jessie's hand. She extended her left hand and seeing the ring, Mr. Strickland jerked mother off the train. He pulled the ring off her finger and turned and threw the ring at my father's feet and said, "Never sir, never. We are even sir. You saved my life once and you will not take it again. Jessie is ours. You understand? Ours!" He turned to Jessie, "Young lady, get in the car!" She felt a hand grab her from behind. She looked and years later she said she still could remember the glint off of the badge of police chief Shifflett. No more words were spoken. A suitcase was picked up and the two policemen let go of my father and the train started up. The steam sprayed out on my Dad's feet as he laid on the platform. He got to his feet, spied the wedding ring on the platform, picked it up, held it in his hands and turned and walked, suitcase in hand, across the footbridge to Sears Hill and his Aunt Vivian's house.

The news of what had happened at the train station spread across Staunton like wildfire. It was said that Mr. Strickland had pulled a gun on Luther Brown and had shot him. Another version had Jessie screaming at her father and having been physically removed to her father's car.

Whichever version one would hear, Luther Brown was seen as the villain. This wonderfully honest, principled person had to walk down Beverley Street to go to work. Every shop window held a face or two and dad marched right downtown and not one person spoke to him or hailed him.

"I can't believe it!" was the most frequently repeated remark when someone would hear a version of what had taken place.

Father opened the door to the Banner Store and was surprised to find that Mr. Davis was already there. Usually Luther was the first to arrive. This morning however, his boss was in first.

"Morning Mr. Davis." "Morning Luther" was all that was said initially.

Then Mr. Davis turned around and said "Luther, I need to hear your side of the story about what happened last night."

My father spent the better part of an hour telling his version of what had happened. About Jessie, about what had happened in Hyattsville and all the rest. No customers had come in, but as Dad looked up, he saw the "Closed" sign in the front door window that Mr. Davis had put there after my father had come in.

If Mr. Davis was expecting an apology for Luther's behavior, he got it. If he wanted to be told that he realized that Mr. Davis had warned him about getting involved, he got it.

Mr. Davis' response to the whole thing was rather muted. Finally he said, "Luther, come with me." And with that, he led the young man to the back of the store and up the back stairs to the building's second floor.

The second floor was used for storage and was filled with tables, bolts of cloth, hatboxes, and such. Mr. Davis pulled the drapes back from the side window and the morning light filled the room. Luther put his hand in front of his eyes to block out the bright sun and could see directly across the street that it was already 9:15, as he was facing the Town Clock Tower.

"Luther, I have been thinking about branching out and offering more services at the store. Really becoming more of a furniture store and providing home decorating services to our patrons. That Venetian blind machine over there is just the beginning, Luther. I want to be able to sell carpets, furniture, and custom upholstering."

Dad listened and then Mr. Davis did more for my father's confidence than anyone had ever done. "And regardless of how this thing with the Stricklands works out, I want you to run this part of the store." He said.

Others would come forward with their endorsements as well; his church, his aunt Vivian, his cousin George, Shorty Minter and the rest of the Beverley Street business people that dad had worked with. What he found out in the days that followed was that people had seen how hard he had worked, what a good man he was and when he needed them, they were there for him. He would go on to work 28 more years for Mr. Davis, first at the Banner Store and then later at Mr. Davis's second store, the larger Augusta Furniture Store. He would become a deacon in the First Baptist Church and live to have his oldest son, Charlie, come back from serving in the Air Force to serving with him in an Easter Communion service in the spring of 1950.

I was always amazed at his ability to read people and analyze problems. He was sincere and honest to a fault. As a Baptist, he never drank, couldn't dance and I never heard him cuss.

He kept his brood of six boys together by being an example of what we all could be.

As for mom, she would say it would take four straight weeks of crying on her part (a record for her, she said) before her foster father, Douglas Strickland, finally realized that this strong-willed young woman was going to do what she was going to do. He helped dad get their first place, a two bedroom walk-up apartment over the Johnson Electric Store on Central Ave. across from the Kasco Ice Plant.

My mother would say that she was happier in that little place of her own than she had ever been. A series of children would follow; Charlie, Billy, Jack, Paul, Jimmy and finally me in 1940.

People would talk about seeing the "stair-step" Brown boys following their father up Lewis Street as they walked to church in those early years. My brothers would have to endure countless moves during those terrible 20's and 30's because of the economics of the times. But my dad and mom somehow would always be able to keep it together. And by the time I came along, we were doing better than we had ever done.

My grandmother would come back into my mother's life in 1933 when mom stopped one summer day at the Farmer's Market that was always set up under those big trees in the parking lot next to the fire house on Central Ave. As she browsed, she spied some homemade butter at one of the stands and on closer examination, she saw the letters "E. R." embossed on the top. The woman manning the table looked up and asked if there was something she could help her with. My mother looked up from under her hat and saw the kind, sunburned face of this farmer's wife. Mom asked if the butter had been churned that week. The woman told her "Yes" and then my mother asked, "What does that E. R. stand for that's on the face of the butter?" The older woman smiled and those weathered laugh-lines appeared on her cheeks. "Well, my brother, Ed, would tell you it stood for his name, Ed Rohr, but that wouldn't be right. You see, that butter mold was my mother's, made for her by her husband James and that "E. R." is for

Elizabeth Rohr, her name." she said. After asking the price, which was more than mom could afford, mother thanked the woman and continued to browse the other stands.

Something grabbed at my grandmother. Maybe it was one of those strange powers she had but it tugged at her heart as the young girl with the empty basket walked away. Maybe it was the way she walked, the way she talked and then it hit her. The basket. She knew that basket. It was the one that woman and man used to carry when they came to buy produce at her mother and father's house. Grandmother left her stand and went over to where Andy Anderson, a fireman, was leaning against the wall. "Excuse me," she said. "Can you tell me the name of that pretty woman with the hat over there?" With that, she pointed at my mother. "Yes mam, I know who she is. That's Mrs. Luther Brown, she and her family live right around the corner on Lewis Street." Mrs. Brown," my grandmother said. "And what would be her first name?" she asked. "I think her name is Jessie, mam. Yeah, that's right, Jessie is her name." The name went through my grandmother like a shot. Through tearing eyes, she made her way back to her stand, picked up one of the pound pats of butter and wrapping it in wax paper, she tied it with a brown cord and headed across the parking lot. As she closed the distance between herself and the younger woman, my grandmother wondered what would she say? How long had it been? What could she say?

What she did say was, "Excuse me." My mother turned and was surprised to see this woman she had just met standing behind her with her hand on mother's arm.

"I just wanted you to have this free sample of our butter, young lady. We do it every once in awhile. My brother, Ed, says it's good for business."

My mother's eyes stayed locked on my grandmother's face as the butter pat changed hands. "No, you don't have to do this." She said.

"Oh, but I want to." The older woman said. Patting the young woman on the hands and turning away she hurried back across the parking lot.

Later that day, my grandmother would get my mother's address from one of the firemen and on returning home, she wrote the most beautiful eight-page letter my mother would ever receive. Visits would follow and mother and daughter would work the next thirty-seven years binding up that love that only an abandoned child and an unwed mother can understand.

Before she died in 1970, my grandmother gave to me her final gift. Although I was now grown and had a family of my own, I found myself at her house out there in the Estaline Valley because they were "doing a hog" and my grandmother wanted to be a part of the butchering "one last time", she said.

It was a cold, clear October Saturday morning and since her husband, Frank Campbell had died, the killing, the stringing up, the scraping and the initial cutting up phase fell to myself, Mr. Kinzer, Mr. Robinson and an assortment of others. Both men and women who all were neighbors of my grandmother and who all loved her.

All the fire building and water boiling and initial cutting took most of the morning and about 9:00 all of the men were called to a big table in grandmother's front yard for breakfast. The young minister from grandmother's church was there and he said grace and then everybody sat down at the "groaning board" of food that had been prepared by the women. "Hoecake and biscuits, home made jam and jelly, the last of the sausage, bacon and enough scrambled eggs to feed the 10th regiment", my grandmother would proudly say. "Washed down with coffee pot coffee with a bit of honey on the side!" I don't remember her being any happier than on that day.

As the day wore on, I took some time away from the work to walk to the springhouse. I pushed open the half door to the old building and made sure the crawdads were still running backwards from my shadow as they did when I was young.

I walked up on the hill behind the house where I had killed so many Indians years ago. I looked down on the green metal-roofed house and could almost hear those voices of boys, now men, who once roamed this place with me.

I can truly say it was just as exciting that day as it had been when I, as a small child, spent those wonderful lightning bug summers with my grandmother.

When I returned to the back porch, my grandmother was washing her hands, having just completed making souse or chitterlings or something. She had taken off her wedding ring and I saw it lying on the bench next to her washing pan. I had never seen her take that ring off before but a lot had happened since last I had been to see her: Her husband, Frank Campbell had died, she had fallen and hurt her hip and now each fall, starting after the yearly butchering, she spent the winter months in Staunton with my mother and dad.

Someone called for her in the kitchen. She muttered something about not being able to see anything in "these infernal glasses of mine." She threw down her towel, finished drying her hands on her apron and pushing the before mentioned gold-rimmed, bi-focal glasses back on her nose, she went into the house.

I picked up the ring. It was very old looking and quite worn. I could barely make out some initials in it and I made my way around the house to read it in the last rays of the evening sun.

It was hard to read, but there they were, two initials, a "W." and a "G." "W. G", I thought, not "F. C. for Frank Campbell, her husband? Who could this be?" And my mind began to race. "Maybe the ring had been given to her by her mother, Mary Elizabeth Glover. Maybe it was her mothers' mother's ring.

If it was her grandmother's ring it could mean that after all she had been put through with her out-of-wedlock, unwanted child, perhaps her mother had, in later years, forgiven grandmother and that was the reason she always wore that ring because it was symbolic of closure for that period of her life.

As I stood there in the half-light, looking at the old ring, I was sure that must be the answer to why these initials were there. I made my mind up to ask her about it at a more appropriate time. That time was never to come but the gift she had given me that day would come full circle years later, after she was gone.

I returned the ring to my grandmother and went back to work on finishing cleaning up her yard. The next day, we closed up grandmothers house for the winter and took her into town to stay the winter at my mom and dad's house. I went back to college, sometimes working three jobs like my father before me, to get that education my grandmother had told me that was so important.

Althea Rowhema Rohr Campbell would die that next spring and would be buried in her beloved Lebanon Presbyterian Church Cemetery, not twenty feet away from the graves of her mother and father.

About 100 people were there to "send her off", as they would say and that night, in her honor, we stoked up that old wood cook stove at her house one last time.

We cooked up some of my grandmother's "hoe-cake" in a frying pan. We slathered them down with homemade butter and finished them off with homemade damson preserves. We sang "Amazing Grace", held hands and hugged and bid grandmother goodbye.

I was the last one out of her little house that night and as I turned off the hall light, I looked one last time at her quilt-covered bed and at the nightstand where her coal-oil lamp still sat. Next to the lamp I could see my grandmother's glasses laying up on her family Bible. Next to that was her sow's ear purse.

Grandmother, at last, had gone home to be with her family.

Epilogue

My dad would live to be seventy, and in an amazing turn of events, spend the last 18 years of his life living at 303 Kalorama St. where he had first seen my mother. Mr. Strickland had died in 1949 and Mrs. Strickland, now very aged, asked mother and dad to move into her big house with her. She would die in 1952.

Around 1972, two years after my grandmother died, I found an old journal I had kept while I was going to college. One of the stories I found there was the one about my grandmother's ring. I had been unable to locate any James Rohr in any death records and I was still attempting to find out where this first husband of my grandmother's had died.

Discussing the "W. G." initials with any of mom's relatives rendered nothing and I could tell that the search for my grandfather seemed to bother my mother.

Finally, a distant relative told me the story of a William Godsey—"W. G", who as a young man, had worked in the Estaline Valley in the late 1890's. A "Handsome cuss he was" this ninety year old woman told me. "The story is that he came from over the mountain near Ivy to cut and haul timber for the railroad camp in Craigsville. Him and Allie, your grandmother, met at a church function and fell in love. One thing led to another and a child, Jessie, your mother, was the result. The story is, he tried to do the right thing by Allie but her father would hear nothing of it and he had the railroad superintendent run Godsey off the job. Only thing I ever heard about this James Rohr person is a story that they made up and later said that he was Jessie's father and that he had died before Jessie ever knew him."

Twenty-one years of hunting resulted in the finding of William Godsey's grave and on a cold, damp morning in April of 1993, I took my mother to see the grave of the father she had never known.

Thus began a four-year reunion with a family she had never seen. Visits to an old cabin where her father had once lived, a picture of an old man in overalls, holding his hat, standing in a field was her only picture of her real father.

My mother died in May of 1997 at the age of 90. In her hand when she died were five pictures of her husband from celluloid collared young man in front of the Banner store to older distinguished gentleman on the porch at 303 Kalorama Street.

She lies, buried in Thornrose Cemetery in Staunton next to her husband and her first born, Charley. She, like my grandmother, had come home to her family. A few moments after her death she was surely on that spiritual highway that leads to Heaven.

There, standing at the Heavenly Gates, Jesus and St. Peter can be seen. Peter turns to Jesus upon spotting this old woman coming up the hill and asks, "Lord, do you know this woman?" Jesus looks and sees her coming and with a wonderful smile on His face, says, "Yes, yes, I know this woman. Jessie is her name."

978-0-595-42391-0
0-595-42391-4

Made in United States
North Haven, CT
23 June 2023

38144137R00064